As Silent as the Night

Danielle Grandinetti

Buon Natale!
Danielle.

Hearth Spot Press

Praise for As Silent as the Night

Riveting from the first scene, *As Silent as the Night* offers a unique, edge-of-your-seat Christmas read. Enter 1930's Chicago where Lucia needs to escape the clutches of a mafia thug and meet Gio, the man who will risk all to find her. Add to that heart-stopping moments of a different kind, and you're left with a beautiful and heart-wrenching romance. Danielle Grandinetti weaves a tale of self-denial juxtaposed with greed, mirroring the same elements in the nativity story that Lucia and her new Wisconsin friends put on. A beautiful, gripping, and romantically suspenseful Christmas story you wouldn't be able to put down if you tried (you won't try)

—Chautona Havig, author of *The Stars of New Cheltenham*

Sweet and suspenseful, *As Silent as the Night* takes readers on a twisty ride that will keep pages turning. Danielle Grandinetti stitches her story together with a theme of belonging and desire for inner peace everyone can relate to. Her captivating characters, heartwarming families, and Christmas traditions aplenty check all the boxes for a fabulous holiday read.

—Beth Pugh, Selah Awards Finalist and author of the *Pine Valley Holiday Series*

Praise for A Strike to the Heart

Strike to the Heart is an entertaining story that grabs you on the first page with its intriguing plot, as Grandinetti expertly balances action with the tender stirrings of a romance that will woo your senses until the very end.

—Natalie Walters, award winning author of *Lights Out*

The romance escalated right along with the winding plot, creating a layered mystery that is sure to delight readers.

—Rachel Scott McDaniel, Award-winning author of *The Mobster's Daughter*

Praise for To Stand in the Breach

Inheritance battles, labor strikes, and a sweet Irish romance to root for ... To Stand in the Breach is the Depression-era tale you won't want to end.

- Kelsey Gietl, author of *Broken Lines*.

A page-turner, To Stand in the Breach combines suspense and romance that leads the reader through a thoroughly engrossing tale of what it means to stand with those you love.

- Ann Elizabeth Fryer, author of *Of Needles and Haystacks*

To my grandparents,
Alfred and Della Grandinetti

Peace I leave with you, my peace I give unto you: not as the world giveth, give I unto you. Let not your heart be troubled, neither let it be afraid.
John 14:27, KJV

And the angel said unto them, Fear not: for, behold, I bring you good tidings of great joy, which shall be to all people.
Luke 2:10, KJV

AS SILENT AS THE NIGHT
Published by Hearth Spot Press
Printed in the United States of America

Kindle Book ISBN: 978-1-956098-04-4
E-Book ISBN: 978-1-956098-03-7
Paperback ISBN: 978-1-956098-05-1

Cover Art: Roseanna White Designs
Author Picture: Abby Mae Tindal at Maeflower Photography
Editor: Denise Weimer

Acknowledgments

There are several people to thank for making this novel possible.

First of all, my friend, critique partner, and fellow historical romance author, Ann Elizabeth Fryer, for reading the rawest version and brainstorming along the way. Denise Weimer, my editor, for helping me craft this book. Lynn Owen, for proofreading. And historical romance author, Roseanna M. White of Roseanna White Designs, for the cover design.

It was also a joy to include various Italian words and phrases. I fondly remember the various Italian words my grandma would drop or the way she and her siblings would sprinkle Italian words into their conversations. It ingrained the cadence of the language into my mind so that when I studied Italian while in Italy one summer, I was able to more quickly pick up the ability to communicate. Despite that background, I wanted to make sure I avoided as many errors as I could, so I am especially thankful to Joi Ehmann for checking my Italian spelling and grammar. Any mistakes or liberties are my own.

Also, thank you to Iron Stream Media, who published *A Strike to the Heart*, where we first meet Gio, and who gave me permission to write this Christmas novella.

Finally, a huge thank you to my husband for encouraging me every step of the way and to my boys for giving Mama a chance to write.

Lastly, but not least, thank you to you, my readers, who have been as excited about Gio's story as I have been! I am grateful to God for each and every one of you.

English-Italian Glossary

Affari – business

Amore — love

Amore ti fa' fare les cose piu' folle — love makes you do the craziest things

Bella signorina — beautiful female friend (miss)

Buon Compleanno — Happy Birthday

Buon Natale — Merry Christmas

Che — what

Coerzione — Duress

Com'è il caffè? — how is the coffee

Come ti senti – How are you

Complimenti. — compliments

Dormi nella pace divina — sleep in Heavenly peace

Dov'è la mia Lucia? — Where is my Lucia?

Fermati! — stop

Grazie — Thank you

Grazie mille — much thanks

La mia famiglia — My family

Mamma mia — an exclamation

Meraviglioso(a) — Wonderful, masculine (feminine)

Mi dispiace — I'm very sorry

Mia mamma — My mother

Mio amico — my friend (masculine)

Molto bella — very pretty

Nipotina — Granddaughter

Notte silenziosa, notte Santa — Silent night, holy night

Padre Dio — Father God

Padrona — mistress

Programma natalizio — Christmas pageant

Punizione — punishment

Ragazza — girlfriend

San Nicolò — St Nicholas

Scusa — Excuse me (informal)

Sei tutto per me — You are everything to me

Si — Yes

Signora — Mrs.

Squisito — excellent

Ti amo — I love you

Tutto bene — all right

Va bene — Okay

Vieni qui — come here

Vuoi sposarmi — marry me

Prologue

November 15, 1933,
Charlotte, North Carolina

Charles "Ice" Connors braced against the car door as their stolen vehicle darted in front of the mail truck before slamming to a stop on the quiet street. In an instant, Ice and the other three members of the crew surrounded the truck. The noonday sun glared down like a spotlight, the trees stood motionless, and the mail driver raised his hands as Dutch shoved a Tommy gun into the man's face.

Satisfied the driver was incapacitated, Ice wiped sweat from his temple. November weather was not meant to be this mild. He circled to the back of the truck, bolt cutter in hand. A quick snap and they were in.

Isaac Costner slapped Ice on the back. "Boss will be happy."

Ice held back his grin and swung himself up into the truck. They hadn't gotten away with the robbery yet.

Inside the truck, bags of money from the Charlotte Federal Reserve waited for them. Ice tossed a bag down to each of his companions, then scouted the truck, searching for a singular item. Owl, Dutch, and Costner returned and Ice tossed down another load to each, per Roger "The Terrible" Touhy's orders. They disappeared around the side of the truck with their loot as Ice spotted the small rectangular box he'd been handsomely paid to retrieve.

Ice waited until the three men took the last of their score to the car—if any of them knew he had an agenda other than stealing the money their boss needed to beat Capone's set up, Ice's body would be left beside the driver's, a bullet hole in his head. But the money! The money made this particular gem worth the risk. He glanced over his shoulder one last time before he snatched the small box and checked the address on the package against the one he'd been given, then slipped the package into his coat pocket.

"Ice, let's go!" Dutch hollered.

Ice grabbed the last bag filled with cash and bank notes, slinging it over his shoulder and jumped to the ground. The box bumped against his thigh, and he resisted drawing attention to it by holding it still. Then he squeezed into the car, the violin case holding the Tommy gun jamming the box corner into his leg and threatening to betray its presence with an unwelcome *bump*.

Outside of Charlotte, they switched to a clean vehicle, then began the long drive back to Chicago. Twisting mountain roads gave way to the interminably straight drive through Indiana before they finally reached the smog-caked factories of Gary and Chicago. Dutch pulled into a warehouse dock on the west side as dusk fell the day after their successful robbery.

Touhy's men unloaded the car as Owl, Dutch, Costner, and Ice received their payment. Then slipped into the night, leaving the car for the others to dispense with. All had gone according to plan, so Touhy should go free despite Capone and his underhanded dealings. Not that Ice cared either way. Not with the score burning a hole in his pocket.

Leaving the drop, Ice slipped around the corner of a building as rundown as the citizens of this windy city. Garbage filled the alley, accosting his nose and warning the less determined to steer clear.

Ice backed into the shadows before he pulled the package from his pocket. A cold wind whistled past him, and he tucked up the collar of his coat, then flipped open his knife.

He slit the package he'd carried from Charlotte. Inside was another box—this one unadorned wood. It slipped into his palm. Ice discarded the original packaging and lifted the lid. Shining back at him was a single, clear diamond set in a gold ring. It sparkled in the fading sunlight, as out of place in the dingy alley as a snow-capped mountain in the desert. Ice ran his finger over the gem. A full carat, he'd been told. For just an instant, he considered dropping it into his pocket and disappearing.

"Do you have it?" A voice stopped him.

Ice turned slowly, fisting the ring. He knew the man, a freelancer who preferred to work for the highest bidder, which currently meant Capone had him doing guard duty at one of his churches. A cushy job. So why was he here?

"The package." The man stepped closer. "He sent me."

He? Ice squinted. The man who'd hired him would want this item returned personally, not through a mercenary. The newcomer's eyes darted to Ice's hand, a gleam betraying that he knew exactly what Ice had been thinking. Before Ice could react, the man raised a hand, and two men materialized behind him, Tommy guns firing.

Ice had no escape. He was dead.

Chapter 1

December 6, 1933
Chicago

Lucia Critelli lowered her head against the bitter wind that raced the cars rumbling down the city street. She'd been standing in the bread line since before first light, and now the rising sun had turned the black sky to a haunting shade of red. A forewarning? She hoped not. She desperately wanted to get a special treat for Nonno on this cold St. Nicholas Day.

Her grandfather had been ailing more than usual, what with their inability to properly heat their apartment. Lucia tried to find work where she could, but half the city was out of work, and jobs were incredibly difficult to come by. Especially for a woman, let alone an immigrant's daughter. Lucia often spent her days in lines like this only to be turned away for not getting to the door before all the food or work had already been disseminated.

Not today. Today she'd bring bread home to Nonno. No matter what.

She raised her eyes to the spire of St. Mark, her destination, the sun gleaming on the cross that rose high above the sooty buildings surrounding it. The rumble of a truck interrupted her silent prayer. She recognized it as it passed her, and when it stopped at the front of the church, a warm, fluttery feeling filled her. Giosuè Vella was delivering supplies today.

Most of the girls in their neighborhood had a crush on the gregarious Italian. Their mammas all tried to create a match with him, and their papas all approved. Yet Gio remained unmarried and seemingly happily so, which meant all the nonnas welcomed him to their table without hesitation, even if it seemed his own mother fed half the Italian community.

With what appeared to be effortless grace, Gio lifted a crate overflowing with fall vegetables from the bed of his truck. Neither tall nor short, his stocky frame seemed to easily carry any type of load, whether physical or emotional. Whenever anyone needed something, Gio was always the man people in their neighborhood went to for help. Somehow, Gio always knew how to find exactly what a person needed, whether the right word, a certain food, or a unique trinket. It made him greatly loved and admired.

And that was the problem. Everyone loved Gio Vella. It made it hard for Lucia to know whether her feelings toward the man were simply the hero worship of the masses or something more. Especially since Gio made her feel special, as special as he made every other person he met.

Stop this! Lucia tucked her chin again and stomped her numbing feet. At twenty-five, she should be well past schoolgirl crushes and pining after a man who obviously had no interest in her, romantically. Right now, she needed to focus on Nonno. Her grandfather was the only family she had left, and she was determined to make sure he knew just how much she loved him before his health stole him from her.

The line moved forward slowly as the sun rose. Its beam hit her squarely in the face as she aligned with an alley across the street, where a newsboy shouted the morning's headline—Prohibition was officially over. The Volstead Act had been repealed. Alcohol was legal once more. Lucia shook her head. What would that do to a city like Chicago?

No need to borrow trouble. Lucia shielded her eyes until the line shuffled her back into the shadows. Gio continued to carry in crate after crate, yet stopped to talk with those standing in line, as if balancing something heavy on his shoulder was no trouble if it meant making someone's day. See! That was what she liked so much.

Lucia muttered to herself in Italian until she realized Gio had also stopped to talk to the two goons standing outside the church doors. Goons who obviously still had a job even though Prohibition had ended. Lucia shivered. Everyone knew they were two of Mr. Capone's men, that even though the mobster was in jail, he kept his empire running. Would that continue after today's news headline? For all his evil, the man also supplied churches with food for people like her, Italians who were out of work and needed a hand. Would this provision dry up as the alcohol flowed legally once more?

One of the thugs caught her staring and flashed her a lecherous grin. With desperation high, Capone's goons provided security for the food he donated. Did that mean Gio was somehow involved with the crime family since he also provided food? She didn't think so, but Gio managed to get things no one else could. And he was talking with Emberto Ettore.

Lucia tore her gaze away before she showed her disgust. Emberto wasn't always at this bread line, but whenever he was, he always showed her unwelcome attention. She had nothing good to say about the man other than for his ability to keep the church's food from being stolen. He could probably read her distaste all over her face, even though she purposefully ignored him as she climbed the steps into the church. His chuckle followed her inside.

The December chill swirled around the hall where the tables of food had been set up. She missed the sun's warmth as her eyes adjusted to the dim interior. The marble and stone echoed the many voices chattering over the free food staples. The woman behind her pressed into her back, causing her to stumble.

"Excuse me," Lucia muttered, ducking her head. No need to draw attention. She, like everyone else, was anxious to get to the tables, praying there would be something left for her. But when the minutes lengthened without the line moving and the chatter grew louder, Lucia rose up on tiptoes, her short height now a disadvantage.

"What do you wish to see?"

"Gio!" Lucia's heart skipped a beat as she realized the handsome man stood beside her, a twinkle in his beautiful brown eyes. Heavens, she was as bad as the hungry, addle-pated youths in their neighborhood, dreaming of a wealthy patron who would rescue them from the streets. Even the sour-faced woman behind her didn't protest Gio's presence.

"There is plenty today." He stuffed his hands into his pockets, his wool coat flopping open to reveal a faded blue vest. "Your nonno, how is he? I have not seen him in days."

Her heart melted at his concern. "He has a cough, so I've insisted he stay out of the cold."

"He misses the people, *si?*" Gio took a step with her as the line finally shifted.

"He does love to talk with all the neighbors."

Lucia felt the irritated stare of the woman behind her boring into her back.

Gio let loose a heart-stopping grin. "He is … how do you say …" He waved his hands, drawing her attention to him alone.

Happiness bubbled. "People-loving? Outgoing? Gregarious?"

Gio snapped. "Gregarious! That is it!"

Lucia laughed with him. She'd forgotten Gio's English stumbled at times. She was born in Chicago, and though Nonno spoke little to no English, Lucia barely possessed an accent. Most of the parents who had children once they arrived in America insisted their children learn

English and only use Italian when necessary, such as when talking to the older adults who spoke no English. Papa was no different before he passed away. However, being an American-born Italian left her feeling as if she belonged in neither world, Italian nor American.

"I have more crates," Gio was saying, gesturing outside. "Tell your nonno, *per favore*, soon I will visit. I wish to see him."

Lucia nodded. If only Gio wanted to see her too.

"Perhaps you ... you will be home also?" Gio squeezed her gloved fingers, then disappeared before she could react, leaving Lucia's face warming despite the coolness inside the church.

Frankly, the man was infuriating. Did he have no knowledge of the heartbreak he left in his wake? And why couldn't she act like the spinster she was? Her life was about taking care of Nonno, as he'd taken care of her. She couldn't let Gio and his winsomeness muddle her head. Or her heart.

She pushed away thoughts of Gio as she reached the table. Opening her bag, she added a crusty loaf of bread, an acorn squash, and two large potatoes. She would make a delicious soup for Nonno to celebrate the holiday. He would be so pleased!

As she turned to leave, she ran into a solid body. Jumping back with a start, Lucia looked up into the bronze face of Emberto Ettore.

"*Signorina* Critelli." The man smiled, but it had the opposite effect on her heart as Gio's smile. Emberto could be considered handsome, as he was taller and broad shouldered, dressed well, and sported a strong jaw that was rarely covered with scruff. But his brown eyes didn't twinkle like Gio's. Any life and light were snuffed out in Emberto's dark orbs.

Lucia gripped her bag. Even with the number of people in the room, no one would interfere with one of Mr. Capone's goons. She raised her chin. "Excuse me, sir."

"I heard your grandfather was ill. You must wish for a way to provide for him."

9

Lucia struggled not to show any response to his words as she attempted to shoulder past him.

"I have a proposition." He winked. "Come with me and we'll discuss it."

Lucia's blood turned to ice. This is what she feared every time she saw Emberto Ettore. One did not say *no* to a man like him, and she knew full well what his *proposition* entailed.

"It is nothing untoward, I assure you. I have need of a messenger. Follow me." He reached for her elbow.

Lucia spun on her sturdy Oxford heels. Skirt swishing against her legs, she dashed for the front door, drawing attention and hopefully Gio's eye.

"Stop running." Emberto grabbed her arm, yanking her into an anteroom.

"I'm not going with you." Lucia tried to pull away, but his grip only strengthened. "I don't want anything to do with your proposition."

His silence was more chilling than anything he could have said. If she didn't get out of the church, he'd make sure she disappeared. However, even if she succeeded in escaping him, he would come after Nonno. What choice did she have but to be his messenger? What did he want delivered?

Gio lifted the last crate to his shoulder and climbed the steps of the church. His breath puffed out in frosty billows as the rising sun warmed his neck. He'd gathered extra vegetables today, hoping to bless as many people as he could for St. Nicholas Day. Seeing the smiles as they spotted the squashes, potatoes, and onions he delivered caused joy to sprout in his heart.

He nodded to people as he passed, but found himself looking for another glimpse of Lucia Critelli. Something about her always lit a feeling he had yet to name. It was a gentle feeling, like the soft light of a candle. It glowed strong, however. Made him work harder when in her presence. Made him wish for a future he refused to seek, especially with someone as innocent as Lucia.

There was no sign of her when he reached the tables, which was odd because she couldn't have passed through the line and gotten past him in the time it took to get the last crate. Now that he thought about it, Emberto Ettore hadn't been at his post outside either, and Gio hadn't missed the look Ettore gave Lucia when she entered the church. Instincts honed from working on the corrupt streets of Chicago and New York, as well as the years as an advance scout for the United States Marines, told him all that information was related and Lucia was in immediate trouble.

Using swift Italian—English took too much effort—he asked those who understood if they'd seen anything. Their lack of reply, their downcast eyes, told him more than if they'd given a perfect report of what happened. Whether because of her beauty or for some other nefarious reason, Emberto Ettore had singled out Lucia Critelli.

There was no way Gio would leave any woman in Ettore's hands—let alone Lucia. He moved from corner to corner, room to room, searching the entire church for any sign of either of them, until he entered an antechamber and discovered Lucia's bag, filled with bread, squash, and potatoes. Food for her nonno. She would not willingly leave it behind unless forced to do so. Or had she known Gio would look for her and left it as a sign only he would understand? No matter, she needed help.

Gio snatched the bag and walked as calmly as he could to his truck. It would do no good to draw attention to himself. He drove around the block and down several streets, but Lucia and Ettore seemed to have vanished. Gio leaned back in the seat of his truck, then tugged off his newsboy cap to weave his fingers through his curly hair. No one actually disappeared. He knew better than most that there was always a trail, if one could find it.

He slapped his cap back on his head and sped toward the Critelli home. Gio built his reputation on the ability to find anything. Today that would include Lucia. He had no doubt he'd find her. Eventually. He always did, especially in the city he knew so well. He had too many contacts, too many eyes willing to see for him, too many ears who would tell him what he needed to know. For the right price. And going up against Ettore would require a steep price.

But first, he needed to make sure Lucia's nonno was safe.

Gio took a turn too sharply, and his tires squealed. He forced himself to slow. Once again, drawing attention would do no one any good. He needed to stay in the shadows, work in the silence, like he had always done. That would allow him to get to her nonno without anyone realizing why he needed to smuggle the man to safety.

Lucia would do anything for her grandfather, like standing in a bread line guarded by a thug like Ettore. Or willingly go with the goon. And it would appear that way to everyone else, especially if Ettore threatened her grandfather, which he likely did. It made the most sense with the information Gio had. Lucia might believe her nonno's life was in danger, but it wouldn't be if Gio had anything to do with protecting him. And he knew just the way to make sure Ettore couldn't touch Lucia's nonno.

Gio drove past the Critelli apartment, checking for anyone watching the place. All seemed quiet. Not *quiet*, exactly, not with kids playing in the street, dodging his truck as they waved at him. Or women talking together on the sidewalk. Or men returning home after another failed attempt at finding a job. But quiet from any unwelcome visitors.

He braked as a boy darted after a ball that bounced in front of him. It slowed him enough to spot the huddle of older boys halfway down the block on the left. He inched forward, careful of the kids playing ball. There, tucked into a crook in the alley, a girl was cowering.

Gio jammed his truck into park, grabbed his knapsack, and jogged across the street. One of the older boys gave a shout, and before Gio could reach them, let alone lecture them, they fled like rats, leaving a curly-headed girl staring up at Gio with tears streaking her face. Gio's heart ripped right in two. He recognized the girl. Her papa had just been laid off and the family evicted. Gio'd lost track of where the family had gone.

He knelt beside her. "*Ciao*, Benedetta. *Come ti senti?*" He scanned her eyes, attempting to discern exactly how the little girl fared. Her slow blink caused a fat tear drop to roll down her cheek. Gio brushed it away, then dug in his bag. That perked her right up. With a grin, he presented her a loaf he'd planned to take home to Mamma. Mamma would understand when he told her why, for the umpteenth time, he failed to bring home bread.

Benedetta bit into the loaf as if she hadn't eaten in days. Gio waited for three bites, fighting the urgency to find Lucia in an effort to make sure this child ate, before asking her about her family.

"Mamma is not well," she explained around another chunk of bread. "Papa and the boys are looking for work." Then she stopped chewing and tucked the rest of the loaf under her arm. The other she threw around Gio's neck. Before Gio could react, the girl had disappeared.

Gio sat back on his heels to collect himself before returning to his truck. If only he could provide everything families like Benedetta's needed. They came to America in hopes of a better future, one away from the hunger and danger of their homeland. They worked hard, fought for every penny they earned, only for this new land to fail them too. He wanted to drive down the street, tossing bread and vegetables to every child, but right now, he had to focus on just one family.

After encircling them with a prayer, Gio pushed Benedetta's family from his mind and returned to his truck. Another two blocks and he parked along the curb. He hurried up to the Critelli home, a second story apartment, his heart pounding in time with his steps and with his fist as he knocked at the door.

"Gio!" The older man welcomed him. Silver hair curled around his ears, a cardigan hung unbuttoned from his shoulders, a grin showed his delight, though it faded as he glanced over Gio's shoulder. *"Dov'è la mia Lucia?" Where is my Lucia?* A dagger wouldn't hurt as much, Gio was sure.

"Ugo, we must hurry. Lucia is in trouble," he replied in rapid Italian. "I'll find her, but first I need you safe. She needs you safe."

The man nodded, fear darkening his eyes.

Gio gathered up necessary items, putting them in the bag Lucia had taken to the church in an attempt to disguise the fact he planned to keep Ugo at his family's house overnight. Gio or one of his brothers could sneak back into the apartment for more supplies, if necessary, but Gio honestly hoped he'd have Lucia back before nightfall.

Shouldering the bag, Gio locked up and helped the older man into his truck. Ugo hadn't asked for details, and Gio filled him in as much as he thought wise—too much information could be deadly when dealing with people like Ettore—but Ugo needed to know the level of danger to both himself and Lucia.

"You will bring my Lucia home?" Ugo rested a leathery hand on Gio's arm. "I cannot lose her."

Gio parked in front of his own family's home, a one-story frame house. The weathered boards contained two bedrooms and three generations, plus whatever guests joined them. Gio turned to the older man. "I promise, I won't rest until I have the answers we need."

Ugo shook his head. "That is no promise, young man."

"I can't promise positive outcomes, Ugo. You know that."

"But you care for her. Do not deny it. I see it in your eyes."

Gio pressed his thumb and forefinger into his sockets, as if he could gouge out the evidence. "I know you want us together, Ugo, but I can't marry her. I'm not the right man for Lucia. She needs someone who hasn't seen or done all the things I have. She is light and I am ... not."

Ugo patted Gio's cheek as if Gio was but a youth. "Do not discredit yourself, young man. She needs a man like you."

Gio let the words go. Ugo had been saying them for years. Sure, Gio had a different respect for Ugo than for the other matchmaking mammas and nonnas. Ugo had a different motive. Gio knew that, yet ... Ugo couldn't possibly understand how bad of a choice Gio was for Lucia. So Gio did nothing.

However, the protectiveness he felt for Lucia and the respect he had for Ugo also meant he had more motivation to find Lucia than any of the other young women he'd been asked to find over the years. Because if he was denying Ugo's happily ever after to save Lucia from himself, there was no way he'd let someone like Emberto Ettore extinguish Lucia's light and destroy her grandfather in the process.

Chapter 2

Lucia supported herself with a hand on a crate as Emberto pushed her into a darkened warehouse. Cold seeped into her bones, and she tugged her worn coat tighter around her shoulders. A mouse skittered over her toes, and the wind whistled through a grungy, cracked window. Lucia shivered.

"Sit by the others." Emberto pointed to a corner shrouded in shadow.

Lucia stumbled that way, weaving between casks and crates and boxes. The closer she came, the more the noises became distinguishable. Women. Young women. All huddled together. Women with dark hair and faces of varying shades of brown. Languages she recognized and some she didn't.

"Speak English?" Lucia whispered to the girl she sat beside.

The woman shook her black curls. "*Nu. Română.*"

Romanian?

"And you?" Lucia looked past the Romanian woman to the one with lighter skin but similar frizzy black hair. "Do you speak English?"

"*Ne.*" This woman shook her head as well. "*Český.*"

Bohemian? What was Emberto up to? She pointed to herself. "Lucia. *Italiano.*"

That received unfriendly looks from most of the girls.

"Why are you here?" Lucia asked in English, then again in Italian, hoping someone would understand her.

A young woman from the back of the group crawled forward. She had striking blonde hair and an angular face. "I am *Polskie*. Małgosia. I speak English."

Relief eased the tension in Lucia's shoulders. "Please, tell me why you're here. What does Emberto Ettore want with you?"

The disdainful looks morphed to ones of pity before Małgosia continued speaking. "We are all from the old country. No family here. No home. No one to miss us. Now Emberto plans to use us." She shuddered. "See?"

Nausea rolled in Lucia's stomach. "We have to stop him or at least get you out of here before he returns."

"You are one of him." Małgosia didn't speak angrily, though there was an edge to her voice. "You are Italiano."

Emberto appeared out of the dark and everyone froze. Without a word, he grabbed two of the girls. They fought him, but a cuff to the head of one silenced both so that they followed him out of the warehouse.

"Girls have disappeared from our communities for years," Małgosia explained. "What can we do?"

Lucia had no answer, but when Emberto returned for two more girls, Lucia stood up, blocking his path. If she was Italian like him, perhaps he would listen to her.

"Move." He pushed her aside.

She grabbed his arm. "Leave them alone."

Emberto laughed. He swung his free arm, smacking her head and knocking her backward. Her foot caught on a box, and she landed squarely on a wooden barrel. Pain radiated through her body, but she pushed to her feet.

"You can't do this." She stepped between him and the girls again. "You are kidnapping them."

Emberto smacked her aside as easily as shoving open a curtain. She tumbled into a pile of crates, and a wooden edge struck her temple.

Dazed and sore, she fought to get her head to stop spinning. The darkness pressed in and the nauseous feeling intensified.

And then Emberto was gone, taking two more girls with him. Lucia faded out, waking only long enough to recognize that Małgosia stayed by her side, a cool hand on her forehead, until Emberto pulled her away too. Lucia could no longer keep her stomach from revolting, but no one was left to care.

"Your turn." Emberto yanked Lucia to her feet. His hands rested at her waist, half holding her up. His fingers slipped to her hips. Lucia pressed a hand to her head, the other to her mouth, and Emberto gave her space. "Straighten up or I'll plug your grandfather."

She couldn't fail Nonno like she had the girls from this warehouse, but putting one foot in front of the other was difficult enough. What could she do? Emberto draped a huge fur coat around her shoulders and stuffed a fur hat on her head before tucking her under his arm.

"Let's go. We need to walk."

Like a lamb led to the slaughter, she went willingly. Because what choice did she have? If she wanted to protect Nonno, she had to go along with Emberto. If only she felt sturdy enough on her feet, perhaps she could get away. Then what? She and Nonno would have to go on the run. Nonno would never survive that.

The cold December air smacked Lucia's face. The bright noonday sun shone through the clouds in splintered rays. The rumble of cars as they chugged by vibrated through her sore head. People passed by and Lucia thought to call out—until she felt the cold, round cylinder of what must be a gun pressed to her side.

"Draw attention and I'll kill you right here."

Lucia nodded. She understood. No one would spare her dead body a second look if she fell victim to a mobster's bullet. Not in this neighborhood.

Down two streets, around a corner, down another street, through an alley, and up another street. She tried to keep her sense of direction, but the dizzying turns mystified her. Just as she spotted the empty blue of where Lake Michigan would be to the east, something latched onto her arm, jerking her away from Emberto. She was spun into an empty alley—alone—as the sound of bone smacking bone cracked through the air.

"We must hurry." Gio Vella snatched her hand and tugged her deeper between the two tall structures. He'd saved her! Merciful heavens, Gio had saved her.

Into the bright sunlight he took her, forcing her to focus on their escape in order to stay on her feet. Faster they went, slipping through smelly alleys and dodging clumps of pedestrians. Her head pounded. Her body screamed with each step. Gio kept a tight hold on her hand, holding her up in their flight.

Finally, he pulled them into another alley and stopped. Lucia's chest heaved with each breath.

"We must remove the coat." He yanked the fur from her head, then helped her out of the coat before pushing them into a trash can. A fierce light shone in his dark eyes and her heart threatened to fall into hero worship.

The chill wind cooled her thoughts, and Lucia shivered. She still wore the coat she'd had on while standing in the bread line that morning, but the fur had been unexpectedly warm, and now she was cold. So very cold.

Gio wrapped his calloused hand around hers, sending warmth shooting up her arm, and silently directed her out of the alley. How she wanted to revel in the hope that he cared for her, had rescued her because she was special to him. Reality swept in on another frozen gust. This is what Gio Vella did. He found things. People.

As recently as October, rumor had it that he'd helped find a farmer's daughter in the middle of Wisconsin. The woman had been kidnapped, just like Lucia had been, and he rescued her. Lucia couldn't read any more into Gio's help. She needed to stuff the unwelcome feelings and simply be grateful he had been able to find her.

They didn't slow again until they reached the crowds on Michigan Avenue. Then, as suddenly as he had whisked her away from Emberto, Gio tucked Lucia under his arm. Lucia braced herself to ignore the feelings that filled her. She spotted another couple acting similarly. This was Gio's way of blending in. If this is what it took to rescue her and keep Nonno safe, she'd willingly risk her heart in the process.

Only ... "This isn't the way home." Panic had her pulling away as they wove around a cheery group of young women strolling with shopping bags hanging from their arms. "We need to get Nonno before Emberto or one of his goons hurts him. Gio, per favore."

"Your nonno, he is safe." Gio's deep voice soothed like honey on a burn, but his slow pace grated.

"You don't understand." She lowered her voice but kept her distance, Gio's touch too distracting for her fraying grasp on the situation. "Emberto Ettore threatened Nonno. I wouldn't have gone with him if I thought Nonno would be safe. I would have tried getting away from him myself, but I couldn't risk—"

"I know." Gio rested his hand on her shoulder, silencing her.

"You ... know?" Why didn't his words make sense?

Gio gave a warm smile that went straight to her heart. Of course he knew! Gio Vella knew everything. Lucia's cheeks heated. Here she was making a fool of herself in front of the man who occupied her thoughts way too often. Heavens! Hopefully, he didn't know how she felt about him. That would be entirely too embarrassing. She'd be like every other silly schoolgirl in the neighborhood, and she couldn't bear for him to think that of her. And why wasn't he saying anything?

"If the plan—if we aren't—" Lucia fumbled her words. "Where are you taking me?"

"Honestly? I ..." His jaw clenched, and he tapped the fingers of his right hand on her shoulder as if moving them would help him think.

Wait. She'd never seen him show any form of indecision. It made him ... human. And even more endearing.

Without thinking it through, she caught his right hand with her left and removed his arm from her shoulder, keeping their hands clasped. "You don't need to impress me with your English. I can understand Italian. Just tell me what you're thinking."

He frowned.

She let go of him as if he were a hot brand. "Oh, mercy, I didn't mean to offend you. I—"

"No. No. I ..." Red deepened his dark cheeks, and Lucia found heat rising in her own again. She put more space between them. What had she been thinking? She hadn't been. She'd acted like a schoolgirl instead of the grown woman she was. She cringed at what he must think of her.

However, Gio merely gave her a curious glance, then switched languages. "Honestly, Lucia, I haven't planned out our next step. First, I needed to get you away from Ettore. That was my priority. Once it was achieved, I planned to regroup based on the outcome of the mission. God, He was looking out for us, yes? I have been thanking Him since we left the last alley. Now I will think on a plan, and we will make a decision when we reach my truck. It is just ahead."

"*Va bene.*" The words rolled from Lucia's tongue, her heart full that this man had thanked God for His help rescuing *her*. "*Grazie*, Gio. I—thank you for saving me."

Again he glanced over at her, an odd look in his eyes that brought the heat back to her cheeks. She touched the side of her face, fingers grazing her temple, and winced.

"You are hurt." He was back to English as he leaned forward, grasping her chin to turn her head. Fingers probed the wound, and she bit her lower lip to hold in a hiss of pain.

"I'll be fine." She put distance between them again and forced a smile. Gio's brows lowered and his lips pursed, but then he nodded and tucked her hand around his arm, the picture of a gentleman escort.

The wind blew in off the lake as they continued down Michigan Avenue, and Lucia tried not to show how cold it made her. Gio seemed content in his wool coat and newsboy cap. He must have felt her shiver, however, because he removed his scarf and wrapped it around her neck before tucking her close to his side once again.

Tears smarted her eyes. Did the man not realize how romantic he was, saving her from an evil goon, then tenderly assuring she wouldn't catch her death in the cold? How could he be this way toward her when he had no interest in her whatsoever? His concern for her felt so authentic, so personal. Was she only fooling herself because she needed the comfort? He squeezed her shoulders and rubbed his hand over the arm farthest from him. Did he notice her emotion?

"To hide in plain sight, it is easiest." His voice rumbled close to her ear. "I am sorry to force the appearance of affection. You will be patient? We are nearly at my truck and cannot linger. I think I know what we must do next."

"Nonno. His safety must be our focus."

"He is safe, Lucia." Gio stopped, forcing their fellow pedestrians to flow around them. He bent to catch her eyes. "You understand? Ugo is safe."

Lucia's heart flipped. And for just a moment, she lost herself in his gaze.

Gio smiled that heart-stopping grin of his and resumed their stroll, turning east just before the spot where the Chicago Christmas tree would soon be delivered. The city had first lit a tree twenty years ago, and every year since, Nonno had taken her to see it. It was the highlight of her Christmas, especially after Papa died in the war. Would she see it this year?

"Ugo, he will stay with *la mia famiglia*. *Mia mamma* will care for him, *sì*?"

Of course she would. Mamma Vella, as everyone called her, took care of everyone, and anyone entering her door would leave stuffed like a bird. The woman could make a single pot of soup feed several dozen. No one doubted where Gio got his generous spirit. But ...

"Before you worry for her, no one will touch them." Gio gave her a significant look.

This time Lucia couldn't interpret it. "I don't understand. Emberto Ettore has powerful friends. What can your mamma do against him?"

"*Si, si.* I have the associates too." Gio rubbed his chest, then switched to Italian. "My brother and brother-in-law are both policemen, and my eldest brother is with the Treasury Department. You understand? Even with the repeal of the Volstead Act, he is a Fed."

"If Emberto disregards all of that?"

"My family is under my protection also." He blushed. "I purposefully have avoided any affiliation with only one group, one crime family, or one law enforcement agency, and now have many connections all around the city. Everyone knows that I will help a person regardless of their associates. Equally and without discrimination. It has earned me safety and protection. Ettore cannot bother me or those under my care without angering everyone else."

"That's why you could speak so easily to him this morning." Lucia still didn't approve. The man was a horrible person who hurt innocent and vulnerable women. "Why not distance yourself from all of them entirely?"

Gio shrugged. "I do what is necessary to help our people, the innocents, the children. They are my priority."

"Wouldn't removing Emberto protect us better?"

"Another would appear in his place. It is the way of things."

"But he's using women. He kidnapped me!"

"Shh." Gio turned her away from a group of pedestrians. "This is not the conversation to have here. It is decided. We must go. Now."

"You're avoiding the obvious."

"No. I am putting your safety ahead of your understanding and have decided to take you to Wisconsin."

"I'm not leaving Nonno."

"For his safety, you must. Do you agree to go with me? I do not wish to take you against your wishes. My friends, they will help us."

"But Nonno ..."

"If there is any danger, I will get him out of Chicago. Lucia, you are Ettore's target. We must hide you until he forgets about you. Then you can return."

"I will never be able to return."

"Not as long as Ettore is searching for you. Now we must get you out of sight. Out of state is best, where he has no contacts."

Gio turned them south again, the grand structure of the natural history museum before them. Beside it loomed the aquarium, and beyond that was the relatively newly opened planetarium, visited by hundreds of thousands of people during the World's Fair this past summer.

Opposite those massive buildings sprawled the home of Chicago's football team. Sunday was the last day of the season, and they were hosting Green Bay. It looked like Chicago would play some New York team in the championship game the following week. She knew all this because Nonno closely followed the football team. He claimed it was part of being American. Not that they'd ever ventured inside the museums or even the stadium. Such things lay beyond the reach of most poor immigrants. But would she ever get the chance now?

Gio eyed her as her steps faltered. "Will you go?"

Oh Nonno, what do I do? "What about all your deliveries? The people relying on the food you bring?"

Gio not only ignored her question, he increased their speed. Lucia snuck a glance at him. His eyes were fixed on something she couldn't see, his free hand rubbing a spot on his chest.

"Gio?"

"We need to leave. No protests, Lucia. This is what your nonno would want."

Lucia's heart sank. She had doubts, of course, but the farther they walked, the clearer the reasons for her hesitancy became. What she really wanted was for Gio to choose to protect her for her sake alone, not because it was his responsibility, or because Nonno would wish it, or because he would help any woman who needed help. She wanted him to help her because he cared for her.

Pain pulsed through her body. Girlish. Foolish. Nevertheless, her heart didn't seem to get the message she'd been telling it—for years! Gio didn't care about her any more than he did any other woman, and she better get that through her aching head before her heart was irreparably crushed by the kindest man she knew.

Chapter 3

Somewhere around the Wisconsin border, Gio began to feel his fingers again. What he wouldn't give to have one of the new heater designs that Ford or General Motors were developing in their newer models. His old truck barely allowed the engine heat to filter into the cab. It was better than nothing, even if it left long trips in December's cold weather frigidly miserable.

Not as miserable as usual, though. Not with Lucia Critelli sitting beside him. Albeit silently.

He hadn't known what to say after her question about his deliveries. He still didn't have an answer for her. In October, he'd let his brothers handle things for him while he helped Miles for a few days. What were brothers-in-arms for if they weren't willing to drop everything and go to one another's aid? That's why he had no qualms about bringing Lucia to Eagle without warning. Whether Gio would stay ... he hadn't yet decided, and that indecision was very unlike him.

People depended on him. On his deliveries. He couldn't let them down, but he couldn't leave Lucia to her fate either. What about the other women and children who could be in danger because he took a couple days away from the city? What made Lucia so special that he would sacrifice them for her? Oh mercy, he knew. And his conscience hadn't weighed on him this much since his time in the Marines, which was why he'd left and refused to carry a gun since. A knife, sure—it was useful in self-defense, necessary in today's Chicago. A gun was a weapon for offense, not defense, and Gio wanted nothing to do with one.

Miles Wright knew how he felt, even if the man had kept up his sniper work until a month ago. Gio couldn't fault him for wanting to protect the innocent doing what he did best. Gio just couldn't do it anymore. But was he any better for leaving his post to help Lucia? For bringing her, but none of the others he'd helped over the years, to Miles?

He could lie to himself and say it was because he respected her nonno. Ugo Critelli was one of the few men who held his complete admiration. The man left southern Italy at the turn of the century with his son Teodore, having buried his wife after disease and famine destroyed his farm. They settled in Chicago, where he attempted to build a new life. According to the story Ugo told him, Teodore married a fellow immigrant who died during childbirth and then Teodore died in France during the Great War, leaving Lucia an orphan.

When Gio met Ugo after Gio returned from Europe after the war—after Mamma moved the family from New York to Chicago—he felt a kinship with the man who lost his son to the same war he'd barely survived as a raw youth, having faked his age and landed in France on his sixteenth birthday. How else was he to escape the awful tenements in New York City? He'd had no interest in following in his brothers' law enforcement footsteps; he'd been in their shadow for too long already—at least, that was the story he held to.

That had to be why Gio felt a responsibility to protect Lucia. At least, it was a reason he could tell himself.

"How are you doing?" He broke the silence to get out of his own head.

"Good." Lucia answered in English. What language had he used to ask his question? He was more comfortable speaking Italian, even after all these years in America.

"Warm?" Gio asked.

She nodded, adding a small smile. *Mamma mia*, she looked so innocent! He, who in years, was barely older than her, but in life, might as well be ancient, should be ashamed of considering any relationship with her beyond watching out for his friend's orphaned granddaughter. Anyway, Gio didn't think of Lucia as something special. Never had. She was just like all the other girls.

Keep telling yourself that, Giosue.

"Who are we going to see?" Lucia asked.

"*Mio amico*, Miles Wright, and his *ragazza*, er, girlfriend. You will like her. Lily Moore. She was kidnapped in October."

Lucia's eyes widened.

"I do not wish to scare you, only reassure you. She will understand."

"That's where you went." Her words were softly spoken and more statement than question. Lucia kept track of his comings and goings?

"I did assist Miles, si, si. He will protect you."

Lucia frowned. "You will not stay?"

No. The word was within his grasp, but Gio hesitated. He knew what he wanted to do. The selfish thing. And would Ugo Critelli even approve of him leaving his granddaughter with strangers, no matter how much Gio trusted Miles?

You will take care of her? Once you find her. The man had clutched Gio's upper arms as he demanded the answer.

You have my word. Gio hadn't meant his promise lightly, nor had he truly considered the implications of his promise.

For Ugo, then. "I will stay, but not long. I must return to make certain Ettore is finished searching for you."

"Then I can return home?" Lucia leaned back in her seat. "That sounds so simple. Like it will only take a couple of days. Nonno won't miss me too much if I'm not gone long. His health is not good. I cannot be away from him for more than a couple days. Not at Christmastime."

Gio rubbed the St. Christopher that hung on a chain under his shirt. Did he tell her it might take longer than a few days for Ettore to lose interest, deeming it safe for Lucia to return? It all depended on how much money Ettore lost when Gio snatched Lucia away. The larger the amount, the longer Ettore would search.

"Does your family know why you've gone?" Lucia fingered a black curl that hung by her neck.

"Si, si. But I did not tell them where. It is better this way."

They fell silent again as dormant fields and quiet towns rolled by until they finally passed the *Welcome to Eagle* sign. Gio's nerves tightened. He hadn't noticed anyone following them, but danger pressed in like an approaching storm. Last time he'd been in Eagle, the dairy farmers were on the verge of a strike. What if the rift hadn't yet ended? What if bringing Lucia here would put her in even more danger?

He turned off the main street to drive by Mr. St. Thomas's boarding house, where Miles had made his home. No sign of his car. And why would there be? Miles would prefer to spend all his time with Lily. Gio glanced at Lucia, then pinned his eyes straight ahead. He had Ugo to thank for these thoughts intruding into his head. No way would Gio ever saddle Lucia with a man like himself. Never.

He needed to focus on Lucia's safety and getting her settled at Lily's house would be the first step. The second would be to keep a distance so Lucia's heart didn't experience any risk from him. Because he saw the way she looked at him. If he gave an inch, he'd hurt her irreparably. He refused to allow that to happen.

Empty, churned-up fields stretched to the horizon on either side, with randomly placed farmhouses and barns dotting the landscape. Lucia had never seen such open spaces, unless Lake Michigan counted. She'd never left Chicago, and now she wasn't so sure she liked the idea of ever leaving it again. She missed the tight alleyways and closely built buildings. They offered security and a sense of safety these fields did not.

Darkness had fallen by the time Gio pulled off the road and drove between a white, two-story farmhouse and a barn partially built with raw wood, light pouring from the wide, open doorway. Two curly-haired, black dogs raced up to greet them as he parked behind the house. Lucia clutched her hands in her lap. Did she have to leave the car? This was Gio's world. Gio's friends. Would she measure up? Did she even want to?

"Do not worry, Lucia." Gio smiled at her, which made her even more nervous.

When she said nothing, he exited the truck. He hailed someone—or maybe someones? Lucia's courage deserted her completely. Why could she stand up to Emberto, but felt terrified to meet Gio's friends?

Her door opened, cold swept in, and Gio stood there, hand extended. If she got out of his truck, the fact that Gio had whisked her away to safety while leaving Nonno behind would be real. How could she have allowed it? She deserved every bit of censure levied by Gio's friends. Concern flashed in Gio's eyes, but he didn't move. His hand held steady. He didn't urge her impatiently or reach for her. He didn't give up and walk away. He stood there. Patient. Understanding. Until, finally, Lucia rested her gloved hand in his.

He lifted her to her feet and held her hand a moment longer than necessary.

Lucia pressed her shoulders straight and raised her chin, prepared to meet Gio's friends and their judgment of her. She wasn't prepared to be met by the dogs first. Well, one dog. The curly head reached her thigh, and its nose pressed into her hand, as if demanding to be petted. She obliged, moving her hand from his muzzle to up behind his ears, the movement soothing her overwrought spirit.

"That's a good dog," she told him. "And what's your name?"

"Smokey." A woman's voice brought Lucia's head up. Illuminated by a lantern, the lady wore her brown hair in a long braid and sported a large flannel shirt, and ... jeans? This was Lily? She rested a hand on the head of the other dog, who sat on the woman's foot while watching Lucia with intelligent brown eyes. "And this is Pieter."

"*Giglia*!" *Lily*. Gio left Lucia and opened his arms. The woman stepped into his embrace. Then, planting his hands on her shoulders, he kissed both of her cheeks. "Let me see you. You look"—Gio sighed as if all was good in the world—"*Molto bella!*"

The woman laughed. "Grazie, mio amico."

Lucia fought to keep her eyebrows from rising. The woman knew Italian?

"And Miles. He treat you well?"

"Very good." A blush rose on the woman's cheeks.

He took her left hand as if examining it. "He propose yet?"

"Gio!" She slapped his arm with her free hand. "It's too soon and you know it."

"It is not. He love you. You love him." Gio shrugged. "Now I am here to see you married."

She rolled her eyes. "Introduce me to your friend, then I'll show you the progress Miles and Joey have made on the barn. I anticipate my first set of new canine trainees on Saturday."

"*Meravigliosa!* It is excellent, Giglia. But Joey and Miles?" Gio's dark eyebrows lifted. "Together they work?"

The woman wove her arm into Gio's and turned him toward Lucia. "You missed the conclusion of my story, but I won't spoil his telling of it. Now, introduce me to your *bella signorina*."

How much Italian did this woman know? And why did she consider Lucia to be Gio's beautiful woman?

"Lily Moore, meet Lucia Critelli." Gio waved between the two women. "Lucia is in need of a place to stay."

Lily squinted at Gio, as if reading into his statement, then cleared her expression to extend both hands to Lucia. "You are welcome to stay for as long as you need, Lucia. The dogs are friendly and will alert us to any danger. You are perfectly safe here."

A myriad of emotions raced through Lucia's thumping heart. Not one of which could she grab onto long enough to feel. It left her mystified and uncertain. This was Working Gio, not her neighbor, not the man she fancied herself half in love with. This man? She wasn't sure she knew this one. He was friendlier with this woman than any others she'd witnessed him interact with. Others he cared for, ministered to, helped. Lily Moore, he respected as an equal, a partner.

"Lucia, you are shaking." Gio was at her side, drawing her toward his chest as if to wrap her in his arms. She resisted and he released her. She couldn't allow his charm to mess with her head.

"Let's bring her inside, Gio." Lily took command. "Have her rest on the sofa, then stoke the stove and put milk in the kettle. I have two jars from my parents in my refrigerator. The chocolate is—"

"I remember, Giglia." Gio wrapped Lucia's arm around his neck and lifted her legs.

Lucia made to protest, but Lily cut her off. "I will get Miles. Perhaps Joey too?"

"He is policeman, yes?" Gio asked.

Lily frowned and shook her head. "Do not ask him. Promise?"

Gio's jaw tightened.

"Fine." Lily rolled her eyes. "Risk your own hide. He might like to even the score."

Beneath Lucia's fingers, heat rose in Gio's neck. It made Lucia's head and heart ache even more. Gio had history with Lily and the people here. History that made Lucia feel ... how did it make her feel? Not good.

Gio carried her through a lean-to, a kitchen with an electric refrigerator and an electric light, through an archway with a rifle hanging above it, to a sitting room with a beautiful fireplace and piles of books. He set her on the sofa facing two wingback chairs before returning to the kitchen, hesitating in the archway as he watched her. The dog, Smokey, had followed them inside and promptly curled up on her lap. Lucia wove her fingers through the dog's fur. How it resembled Gio's hair. Okay, maybe she shouldn't go there.

The back door banged open, and Gio raised his hands as if under arrest. Lucia stared as a man with Lily Moore's same startlingly green eyes stalked up to Gio and pointed a finger in Gio's face. "What problem did you bring my sister this time?"

"Problem?" Gio scowled and batted the man's hand away. "I helped solve Giglia's problem. Or do you not remember the explosive?"

"I also remember the knife you held to my throat."

"You have not forgiven me for that?" Gio shook his head. "Mamma mia, it is in the past."

"He's right, Joey." Lily stepped between them. "No need to be my protector. You know that. And you know Gio is one of the men I trust."

Joey glared at Lucia. "What about her?"

"She has a name, brother dear. If you cannot be civil, I suggest you leave. Or I'll have Miles toss you out." She waved at a bear of a man who came into view, massive arms folded across his chest.

Lucia wanted to sink into the sofa. Their angry words, their scrutiny, their distrust ... of *her*. It hurt. And Gio? What would he say to all of this? Why had he brought her here?

"Ah, mio amico, this is Lucia Critelli. She needs to be away from Chicago."

"I knew you brought trouble." Joey planted his hands on his hips.

Miles frowned. "Who is she to you?"

"My neighbor." The words were delivered quickly, like the jab of a rapier to Lucia's heart.

Lily raised a single eyebrow. "What were the words you spewed to me about Miles? Something about *amore*?"

Gio sputtered.

"Lily is right." Miles's two hands engulfed Lily's shoulders. "You would not have brought her here unless—"

"*Andiamo*!" Gio pushed the large man toward the back door, snagging Joey on his way.

"Just none of you shoot each other," Lily hollered after them. Then came and sat beside Lucia. "I'm sorry. You should not be talked about as if you were not here. It is no better for them to talk about you and plan your future behind your back, but this way I can talk to you without them butting in."

"Thank you, I think?" Lucia's tumultuous feelings eased only slightly at Lily's words. "They won't harm each other, will they?"

"Doubtful. Gio is quickest with his knife, but Miles is not armed today, that I know of." Lily cocked her head. "May I ask? I know I shouldn't, but Gio and you ... are you more than neighbors?"

"No. If he has brought no one else here before, I can't imagine why he would bring me. I am nothing special to him."

Lily pressed her lips together. Her larger dog sat on her foot, and she ran her hand down his back. "I cannot speak for Gio, but from what I just witnessed, I suspect you are very special to him."

Chapter 4

G io wrestled his temper as he shoved Miles out the back door. His words tangled in his mouth, Italian and English mixing as he attempted to express himself. *Oh, Padre Dio ...* Had he been wrong to bring Lucia here?

Miles clapped Gio on the shoulder. "I've never seen you this upset over a woman, Gio. What's going on?"

Gio dragged his newsboy cap from his head and moved his stare from Miles to Joey. Miles stood there with the patience of a sniper and Joey with the eye of a policeman and the lantern. Both would not only wait him out despite the wind whipping across the empty fields, but force him to say what he'd been denying to himself for years. He needed to change their focus and fast.

"*Tutto bene.*" Gio smacked his cap on his thigh and forced his tongue to speak English. "Lucia, she has caught the eye of a dangerous man, Emberto Ettore. He threatened her nonno, her grandfather. I brought her here to hide while Ettore, his memory, it clears." Gio moved his hands to add emphasis to his words.

"She's pretty, so that won't be a short time." Joey rubbed his neck. "And the grandfather?"

"Safe enough." Gio hoped. He could trust his brothers, but their coworkers ... money bought silence, information, and a change in loyalty.

"What's the plan, then?" Miles asked. "Will waiting out this Ettore solve the threat?"

"Doubtful," Joey muttered.

"Is there a defensive position we need to take? An offensive one?" Miles rattled off the words as if he were a commanding officer. "You and I can return to Chicago—"

"No vigilante justice, Wright." Joey stopped Miles's flow of questions. "Gio, have you told the police the problem yet?"

"My brothers, they know what has happened." Gio twisted his cap in his hands. "They plan to go to the warehouse, to do the investigating, but without proof of a crime"—he shrugged—"what can they do?"

Worse, Gio had to stay silent. He couldn't turn in Ettore. The deals he made in order to deliver food to the needy required him to be completely neutral. He couldn't take sides or rat on anyone, or he risked getting a hit taken out on him. He might drop tips to his policemen brothers, but he could never testify. Gio's compromise silenced his mouth so he could fill those of the innocent children who littered the streets of a depressed city.

"Isn't Lucia proof?" Joey scratched his cheek. "Why can't she come forward with what happened to her?"

"You do not understand!" Gio clamped his eyes shut, a prayer winging its way to heaven as he regained his composure. He met Joey's gaze. "Witnesses die, you understand? It is the *punizione*, the punishment, when turning in *il mafioso*."

"Mobster?" Joey's eyes could have popped out of his head. "You've brought *that* type of danger to Eagle? We couldn't figure out my sister's kidnapping. No way can we help your friend. You need to take—"

"The Eagle police can't help, this is true." Miles took a long, deep breath, as if making a decision in that moment. "But we can. I can. I'm trained for this. As are you, Gio. Joey, if you want in, I can supply you weapons."

"You aren't with the Craft Agency any longer, Wright—" Joey never had approved of Miles working for the private security company—"and you have my sister to consider."

"I know she'd want to help." Miles stuffed his hands in his pockets. "And you know your sister well enough to know she would too."

Joey stared at the sky. "So we're going to hunker down here and hope this Ettore doesn't find us? Or maybe hope he does so we can *legally* take him out?"

"It depends on why he chose Lucia." Gio reinserted himself into the debate. As relieved as he was that they'd help, they deserved all the facts. He couldn't minimize the potential danger. "If Ettore wants Lucia for himself, then he will pick another girl. He tires of them quickly."

"Perhaps." Miles scratched his stubble. "But does he know you like her?"

Gio felt the heat rise in his neck. "I hope no one knows."

"If I saw it, why not him?" Joey raised an eyebrow.

Panic rose in Gio's chest. "You are a policeman, of course you—"

"Not anymore," Joey growled.

"*Che!* Why?" Gio poked the bear, but Joey's pointed observation had him reeling.

"My reasons are my own and not relevant to the situation," Joey snapped. "Though I'm glad to have left when I did."

Even Miles raised his eyebrows.

"It's not the strike—it's the Volstead Act," Joey said. "Though it hasn't been enforced in Wisconsin since '29, I don't see how alcohol can be illegal one day and legal the next. The act was an amendment to the Constitution! We spend years locking up offenders, risking our lives policing this law, then suddenly it's okay to serve, sell, and make alcohol again?"

Miles and Gio glanced at each other. Joey must have been stewing on the topic for awhile, but Gio had no idea how to answer. There were many laws he did not understand and the Volstead Act merely allowed the crime families to control the city.

Fortunately, Miles spoke up. "Do you wish they would have left it illegal and allowed the speakeasies to continue?"

Joey waved his hand. "Honestly, I don't know how I feel about alcohol itself. My problem is with turning a law into part of the Constitution and then changing it a few years later. As a policeman, it is disheartening. Now I don't have to deal with it and I'm glad of it." Didn't sound like it.

Silence settled between them, so Gio asked, "And the strike? It is over?"

"I'm not sure it is." Joey sighed. "Tensions are still riding high and my brother-in-law, Andy, is nervous. He's considering hiring extra security in January."

"You think he'll need it?" Miles turned to Gio. "Ever since October's events, things seem calm here in Eagle. There's a tentative truce across the state. It's been in effect since before Thanksgiving. The holidays have made everyone feel more like enjoying a little peace on earth, but I don't know if it will hold."

Peace on Earth. Gio smacked his forehead. "That is right! It is San Nicolò's Day!"

"San what?" Joey scrunched his face.

"Saint Nicholas Day." Gio forced his tongue to say the patron's name in English. "It is a feast day for us. We give gifts. Eat food. It is the day"—he waved his hands, as if he could pull the word from the mind of Miles or Joey—"how do you say ... ah! It is the day Santa Claus, the day he comes."

"Isn't that Christmas Day?" Joey asked. "I mean, I know our community gathers on the twenty-fourth instead of the twenty-fifth for a meal and gifts, but what does the sixth of December have to do with anything?"

"You both are strange." Miles laughed. "We celebrate Christmas on the twenty-fifth like the rest of the world."

Gio couldn't help but smile. "You speak of Christmas, si, si. We celebrate that too. For us, Christmas is many days. San Nicolò Day, that is today, and Lucia is not with her nonno, her grandfather. He is ailing, you understand?" She'd been planning to make him a feast, such as could be in these thin days, and all the more special because of it. Now he'd whisked her away to another state, with people she didn't know. Should he have waited until morning?

"Do not second-guess yourself." Miles put a hand on his shoulder. "Let's make Lucia's first night with us special. What do we need to celebrate this Saint Nicholas Day?"

"It is a day of feasting and gift giving ..." Gio let his words trail off as his thoughts spun with how to do that with so little time. Already evening was pressing in on them. Surely, there would be no harm in waiting until after the festivities to put a plan of protection in place. Ettore hadn't followed him to Eagle—of that, Gio was most confident.

"Lily already planned to make hot chocolate," Miles was saying. "What if I pick up a few peppermints to add to it? With money tight, Lily misses that Christmas treat."

"And Katy and I can bring over some of her root vegetables," Joey crossed his arms, a silly smile on his face as he mentioned his girl-friend. "She always has an abundance because her veterinarian clients often pay her in food, and I know she would be honored to share her bounty."

Gio blinked back the emotion pressing against his eyes. "What can I do?"

"Help Lily bring in whatever game she's put away," Miles said without hesitation. "If she had success this morning, it might be fresh."

Gio shook his head. "You two volunteer this food that is not your own. What will Giglia and Katia say?"

The two men looked at one another. Miles spoke. "He's right. We need to do something special for each of the girls."

"You already suggested the peppermint for Lil," Joey said. "For Katy, I'll pick up her favorite coffee blend. She's been double brewing the grounds lately and hates weak coffee."

"And Gio?" Miles grinned at him, just like a cat would before he cornered a mouse. "What will you get for Lucia?"

Gio's heart twisted. What could he get the most beautiful girl who could never know how much he cared for her?

Miles—the large man who, Lucia learned, was also Lily's boyfriend—interrupted her conversation with Lily when he requested Lily's assistance outside. The dogs followed, and a cloud of loneliness descended on Lucia. She'd planned to spend the day cooking for Nonno. They'd not only enjoy a feast together, Nonno still slipped a coin or some type of treat into her sock every St. Nicholas Day. Fortunately, he'd given up nagging her about circling a pillar seven times or attending the special mass in hopes of changing her marital status.

However, without fail, he'd tell the age-old story of Nicholas of Myra, for whom the feast day was named. Way back in the 4th century, the tale went, the man came upon a destitute father with three daughters. With no dowry, the girls would be sold into prostitution. So that night, Nicholas slipped a coin into the shoes they'd left by the door, enough to keep the girls free. Now children hung socks before the fireplace or set shoes outside the doorway in hopes Saint Nicholas would leave a gold coin for them, too. Lucia always thought it a touching story, but after meeting the girls in Emberto's warehouse, she had to wonder ... if Nicholas was the patron saint of children and women, why had the girls in the warehouse been taken from their homes on his feast day? There had to be something she could do to save other girls before that happened to them.

"Lucia, come help!" Lily's cheery voice banished the dark thoughts forming in Lucia's head.

"What can I do?" Lucia leapt to her feet, but upon entering the kitchen, her jaw dropped as Lily carried in two dead birds with long, colorful feathers. Gio was a step behind with an armful of wood.

"We're making a stew." Lily's green eyes sparked like emeralds. "Katy is on her way with vegetables. We'll dress these and—why are you making that face?"

Making a face? She knew only that her head felt light.

"Oh, Lucia." Gio was instantly by her side, wrapping her cold hands in his warm ones. "You have never seen meat processed, have you?"

Lucia's stomach turned. No, she'd never seen—

She and Nonno did not buy live animals to ... eat. Not even chickens. No, they went to the butcher to obtain their meat—at least, once upon a time they had, on those few days a year they could afford it.

"I will take Lucia for a walk." Gio pulled Lucia through the kitchen, the dogs underfoot, as Lucia struggled to regain herself.

"Have her wear my farm jacket and take the lantern," Lily called after them, then told the dogs to stay.

Gio helped her into the coat, the smell of the outdoors and many animals filling her senses. One step into the cold night air and the world righted itself. Of course, a farm would have live animals raised for food. Where else would a butcher get the meat they ate?

"You will forgive me?" Gio shut the door behind them, his question intruding into her thoughts.

"You did nothing wrong, Gio. I should have expected it." Lucia banished the image of the birds from her mind. "I did not think. We are on a farm. It will be a treat to have meat tonight."

"Hmm." Gio threaded her hand through his arm. "Do you miss your nonno? Pardon, foolish question. I—how do you say—"

"Gio? Would Italian be easier for you?"

"Si, si, but not for you. I wish to make you comfortable." Those brown eyes studied her, yet made her feel warm and safe and—

"Nonno does not speak English, and I am comfortable speaking to him." Lucia offered a shy smile. "Why not you?"

Gio turned toward the trees on the north side of Lily's property the darkness shrouding them like a blanket. "I wish my English is better. I try, but it is ... it is not easy language."

"Do you speak Italian for your work?"

He nodded. "And other languages."

"Other languages?" How did Lucia not know this?

"I must. Chicago has many communities suffering right now. I bring food to as many places as I can. I admit"—he squeezed her hand—"my neighborhood is dearest to my heart."

Nevertheless, a pang that more than their neighborhood lay close to his heart shot through hers. Were there other special ladies in those other neighborhoods? Could he see her as more than a friend? More than his friend's granddaughter? She needed to change the subject. "Do you notice people going missing in any of those neighborhoods you visit? Young women, in particular."

Gio frowned. "What do you mean?"

Lucia told him about the women she met in the warehouse. Their nationalities. What it seemed Emberto wanted with them. All the while, Gio's face grew darker, angry.

"I want to do something." Lucia's shoulders slumped. "But what can we do against Emberto?"

"You do nothing now." The command had iron wrapped around it.

Lucia folded her arms, guarding her heart while missing his warmth. "How can I hide away from Emberto when those women are suffering because of him?"

This time, Gio switched into Italian, and the words rolled off his tongue. "You cannot help these women if Ettore captures you again.

Do you not understand? He will use your compassion against you. Then you cannot be of any help to any of those girls, to your nonno. No, first we make sure you are safe, then, maybe—"

"Maybe?"

"Si, si, maybe. It is dangerous, Lucia. This problem, it is more than Ettore. Stopping him alone will not end the entire problem. I know how bad it is, I see it, and I fear it will only get worse now that the families have lost their alcohol income. But, Lucia, I couldn't bear it if you disappear like one of those other girls."

Lucia opened her mouth but shut it when she realized what he said. He cared about her. Her heart hammered against her ribs, her imagination jumping to conclusions her mind wasn't ready to accept.

"The women, you say they are immigrant?" Back to English now. "And they are alone?"

"Yes." Lucia shut down her wayward thoughts. "That is what they told me. No family to ask after them, to miss them."

Gio rubbed his chest as he had before when he'd seemed uncertain, the gesture at odds with his muscular form, his confident manner. Even at odds with the way he'd jumped into protecting her. "Maybe we work with that. Not now, but we will think on it." That he had uncertainties and weighed the danger made him relatable. And wise.

"Thank you, Gio." She replaced her hand on his arm. "Thank you for caring."

His brown eyes warmed as he smiled down at her. Was it possible he'd stepped closer, the lantern light creating dancing shadows in the contours of his face? Perhaps it'd only been her imagination again, because his gaze passed over her shoulder. In an instant, Gio spun to put himself between her and the house, muscles tense.

Lucia peered around his broad shoulders, spotting two cars parking alongside Gio's truck.

Gio relaxed as three shadowed forms emerged from the vehicles. "It is Miles and Joey and Katy," he said with a smile, his voice warm as one's became when speaking of old friends. Would she ever get the chance to know him and his friends with such familiarity? Or would things go back to the way they had been once the threat of Emberto was neutralized?

Even so, she needed to know more. "Who are all of these people to you?"

"Miles, he saved my life when we first met during the war. He and I were in Marines together—I stumble on his sniper position in *Francia*—and now he is like my brother. Lily is his girl. I help him rescue her in October. Joey is twin brother to Lily, and Katy is his girl. She is veterinarian. They have come to feast with us. To celebrate Saint Nicholas Day."

Lucia's breath caught. "They were planning this already? We've interrupted them?"

"No, no. I told them you planned to celebrate with your nonno." Gio squeezed the hand she still had resting on his arm. "They want to celebrate with you so you do not miss your nonno so much. So you will not be sad."

"They did this for me?" Lucia swallowed. "They don't know me."

"I know you." Brown eyes intently locked with hers. A blink. And Gio looked away again. "I know you will like them, just as they will like you."

"Gio? Do *you* like me?" Lucia covered her mouth. The question had slipped out without permission, but she couldn't be sorry.

"Of course, I like you." Gio would not meet her eyes and huffed. "Lucia, I cannot answer the question the way you want. Many girls have wanted more than I can give them. I wish not to hurt you."

Lucia's heart cracked. "Then you care for me no differently than any of the other neighborhood girls?"

Gio's jaw ticked as he nodded.

"Then why have you brought me here when you have not brought any of the others you've rescued?" Tears smarted. "Why did you tell your friends about Saint Nicholas Day? Why do you care about my feelings?"

"I care about everyone."

Nonsense. Lucia stepped in front of him. "Why have you treated me differently than all the other girls? Gio, I need to know."

Gio lifted his newsboy cap and scrubbed his fingers through his curly hair. "I will not hurt you, Lucia."

"Why are you so confident you would hurt me? Look at what you've done for me tonight. You told me you care about me. You've sought only to protect me. How is this hurting me?" Lucia crossed her arms. "Frankly, letting me think I'm special by bringing me here and refusing to explain will only hurt me more in the end. I know you've treated me differently. Tell me why. Please."

Finally, he raised his eyes. Eyes filled with pain the likes of which she'd never seen in the man before. It caused her to waiver on her feet, hesitating between taking a step forward or a step back.

"Lucia, I cannot."

Hurt lanced deep and Lucia backed away. "I'm sorry. It was forward of me to ask. Your friends are waiting, then I'm sure you must return to Chicago."

"No." Gio grabbed for her hand. "You are right to ask and you are correct. You are special to me, and I will not let Ettore hurt you. I will not let me hurt you. That is why I cannot answer your question. I cannot let you close. I would only hurt you."

"Is that why you have not married?" Lucia's face burned hot, but she refused to back away from the question. They would not have this conversation again.

Gio lowered his chin. "I would only hurt the woman who married me." The pain etched in Gio's features showed just how much he believed that.

"Then why are you a matchmaker? Everyone comes to you for romantic advice."

"Because I am not intending a match for myself, I can see what others want. I see whether love is there, or not. I can nudge or give hope, or provide an alternative when someone needs a different choice. I know people. I have connections. It is a joy to bring happiness to the lives of others."

Drawn into the depth of his words, one more question hovered on Lucia's lips. Dare she ask? Yet it seemed the summary of everything left unsaid. "Gio?" Lucia swallowed, then forced out the words. "Why have you not paired me with anyone? If I am special to you and it is my happiness you seek, then why have I not been a subject of your matchmaking?"

The panic that drained Gio's face of color had Lucia glancing around to see if the cause was external. Because if it was internal ... did that mean his feelings for her went as deep as hers for him?

Gio led Lucia back toward the house in a daze. Thoughts bounced in his head like debris from an explosion. Lucia's questions had set off a charge and Gio couldn't perform triage.

He pressed his hand to the medallion hanging from a gold chain around his neck. The St. Christopher itself held no power, he knew, but physically touching it grounded him and prompted him to pray. Only, now he had no coherent words to bring before his Father. How had he missed Lucia's interest in him? How had he allowed himself to care so much for her? How—

Lucia grabbed his arm. "She's Irish," her voice trembled. "She won't like me, Gio. What if she tells Emberto I'm here?"

Who? Oh. "No. Katy, she would never do that."

Lucia stayed behind him as he greeted Katy, Joey, and Miles.

"Welcome back!" Katy's Irish accent gave her words a lilt. Back in Chicago, the Italians and the Irish were at odds, but not to Gio. He worked among all groups, from his own Italians, to the Irish, the immigrants from Poland and Hungry and Romania, and the Blacks.

"This is Lucia Critelli." He gently brought her forward. "She came here for refuge."

"Och, I can understand." Katy grasped Lucia's hands. "You are safe here, ya hear? These three, they will make sure no one can find ya."

Lucia nodded, but Gio sensed her hesitancy.

Katy speared Gio with a sharp look. "Does she have a connection to you?"

"Connection?" Gio frowned, his mind scrambling. "We are not—"

"Right. I suspected as much." Katy grabbed Joey's arm. "She stays with me. Tomorrow we move her—first thing—so he cannot find her."

"Why?" Lucia demanded. "How do you know who's chasing me?"

"There be only one reason you need protection from three men such as these. I know, believe me."

Gio's shoulders sank as he met Miles' eyes. Katy's words sank in, clearing his confusion. He hadn't been thinking—none of them had—and certainly not like a woman who had been hiding for years, escaping across an ocean to hide from the man who threatened her.

The jarring reminder brought one thing into focus: he needed to re-turn to Chicago at once. Lucia not only muddled his mind, he couldn't allow Ettore to trace her here through him. Her safety required him to put distance between them and to leave her protection in the hands of Miles—and God.

Gio pressed the St. Christopher against his chest. First, they would celebrate Saint Nicholas Day together and now he knew exactly the gift he would give her.

Chapter 5

Thursday, December 7

The next morning, Lucia found herself in Lily's truck, being moved to Katy's house while Gio returned to Chicago to "make an assessment." Those were the words he used, but Lucia had to wonder if he was running from the bold questions she asked him yesterday.

"Mrs. St. Thomas is in charge of the Christmas pageant on Saturday and the Christmas Eve nativity." Lily tapped a rhythm on her steering wheel. "She insisted that Katy and I provide two trays of cookies. She likes Miles, and Katy, and I think this is her attempt at being nice to me." She flashed a grin.

Lucia didn't understand the dynamics, so she steered the conversation toward what she did know—baking. "What type of cookies will you make?"

Lily shrugged. "Katy and I are going over to Mrs. St. Thomas's boarding house this afternoon to use her oven. She has one of those newfangled electric ovens and all the ingredients. She just needs hands to make the cookies." Lily glanced at her. "Would you like to join us?"

Lucia considered the invitation as Lily pulled into Katy's yard. Before she could give an answer—*no* was on the tip of her tongue—Katy exited her barn to meet them. "Welcome to me home, Lucia!" The woman's Irish brogue rolled from her tongue, and Lucia fought off a shiver.

When she'd first heard Katy's accent last night, she had nearly run from Lily's house, despite Gio's assurances. In Chicago, Italians and the Irish did not get along, and the possibility of trusting an Irishwoman only caused her fear to deepen. But Gio trusted the veterinarian. He must, right? Why else would he have agreed to her staying here instead of at Lily's house as originally planned?

"Tell Lucia she needs to join us at Mrs. St. Thomas's." Lily grabbed the satchel she'd filled with the garments she'd loaned Lucia until Gio returned with some of Lucia's own clothes.

"Yes, yes, you must." Katy's grin lit up her dark ensemble. Dark hair, dark dress. Why did Gio trust her, again? "Mrs. St. Thomas has an electric oven that I love to use."

"See?" Lily laughed. "I'll put your things inside, Lucia. You will join us, right?"

Lucia must have nodded because Lily vanished into the house. Katy cocked her head and Lucia felt her study. Instead of pity, however, Katy's eyes showed sadness and compassion. Could Lucia have found someone who truly understood, an Irishwoman no less?

Without Gio here, Lucia felt lost. What connection did she have to these people, as kind as they seemed? Miles and Joey obviously loved Lily and Katy. The simple gifts they'd bestowed last night had caused the women to shine like shooting stars. Gio had given Lucia a St. Christopher. Based on the significant look Miles and Lily had shared with one another, there was a story behind it, but Gio had said nothing about it. And now he was gone.

"I must first close up my barn. Come help me." Katy turned, leaving Lucia no choice but to follow if she wished to hear the rest of the woman's words. "I do not keep many animals, ya see. Just me horse, Clover, me donkey, Glenn, and me dairy cow, Nessa. I get too many eggs and smoked pork as payment for my veterinary services, so no need to have chickens or pigs."

Lucia nodded along with the commentary, but her thoughts snagged on one animal in particular. "You have a donkey?"

"I do." Katy pushed open the barn door and pointed at the middle stall on the left. "Glenn helped me plow me fields until Clover joined us."

Lucia passed the black-and-white cow—while eyeing the massive black horse in the far stall—and slowly approached the middle pen where a gray donkey lifted its nose over the gate, its long ears perked straight up. "He's cute."

The donkey replied with a bray, showing big, square teeth.

Katy laughed. "He likes ya. Glenn, he is me early warning signal."

"Is that why Gio wanted me to stay here?" Lucia pressed fingers to her mouth. "I'm sorry. I should not have said that aloud." What was wrong with her? These annoying questions kept slipping out and ruining everything. She should be grateful to have a place to lay her head.

Katy stood beside her, rubbing Glenn's nose. "I believe all three of our men thought it best."

"Our men?"

A twinkle lit her dark eyes. "My pardon, then. I only assumed he is yours, since he is as watchful of you as Joey is of me and Miles is of Lily."

Lucia clamped her lips together to keep another question from popping out. Like, why couldn't Gio see what everyone else saw? That he treated her differently because he cared about her. It muddled a girl's head.

Katy's hand on her arm stilled Lucia's thoughts. "The reason they wish you to stay here is because I have no easy connection to you or Gio. If someone knows of Gio's friendship with Miles, they may think you will stay at Lily's home. I know it is difficult to trust a stranger, but you are welcome."

Lucia blinked. It must indeed be Christmastime for an Irishwoman to treat Lucia with so much kindness.

"All ready?" Lily's voice traveled from outside.

"Will ya join us?" Katy didn't move, waiting for Lucia's answer.

She wouldn't have before, but now? Lucia patted Glenn on his head. "I would like that. Thank you."

In no time, Lily and Katy pinned Lucia between them in Lily's truck. The women talked of people Lucia had never heard of, though she began to piece names together, such as Lily's parents and her brothers and sister. One sister—Amy—recently married the dairy processing center owner, Andy Booth. Two youths from opposing families marrying in the middle of a violent strike? How could *that* end well? Yet it seemed Gio had a part to play in the happy ending. Typical. She needed to ignore that wistful twisting in her chest, that missing him. No matter what anyone else thought.

A gray-haired woman greeted them at the front door of a multi-storied house. "Who have you brought with you?" Spectacles hung from a chain around her neck and, at first glance, Mrs. St. Thomas seemed a frail old lady. However, the spark in her eye as she assessed her visitors betrayed the fact that Mrs. St. Thomas remained as sharp as a needle.

"This is Lucia." Katy handled the introductions. "She will make cookies with us." Mrs. St. Thomas nodded at Lucia, eyed Lily, then waved them inside a home filled with all sorts of knickknacks, doilies, and other homey bric-a-brac.

"Wait until you see the oven." Katy followed Mrs. St. Thomas, speaking over her shoulder as she led the way into the kitchen. "You set a temperature and don't have to feed it with wood. Isn't that revolutionary?"

"Yes, it is." Mrs. St. Thomas chuckled. "But I wish you would visit more often to use it."

The kitchen was modern and bright. Mrs. St. Thomas made good use of her electric, what with the electric light, the electric refrigerator, and the electric oven.

"Now that winter has arrived, I will, I promise." Katy snatched a booklet from the well-used table and waved it at them. "See this recipe book? Too many choices!"

"Like what?" Lily leaned over her friend's shoulder. "Oh, ladyfingers!"

"Make the sugar cookies." Mrs. St. Thomas set a sack of sugar on the table with a thump. "I need to run over to the church. Send Miles if you need my help. Katy, is it still okay to use Glenn for the live nativity?"

Katy laughed. "Glenn would not miss it for the world. Have you found a new Mary now that Amy is married?"

"Mrs. St. Thomas refuses to cast a married woman in the role," Lily whispered to Lucia. "My baby sister has been Mary for the past five years, so it's quite the discussion around town."

"I haven't yet." The older woman sighed. "I wish you would agree to it."

Katy took a step back. "I could not, Mrs. St. Thomas. I must keep watch over the animals."

"I know, dear."

"What about Lily?" Katy hid her nose and mouth behind the recipe book. "She would be a wonderful choice."

Mrs. St. Thomas's eyes widened and Lily sputtered.

"What?" Mirth sparked in Katy's eyes. "I know ya both are not fond of each other, but Lily is not married. Yet."

"Hmph. I really must be off." Mrs. St. Thomas bustled out the door. "Clean up after yourselves, ya hear?"

Katy waved goodbye with a laugh. "You Moore twins sure do have a reputation around here. It is a good thing ya have Miles and me to run interference."

Lily crossed her arms. "I don't know what you were thinking, planting that idea in her head. I would never make a good Mary."

Suddenly, two sets of eyes turned on Lucia.

"Oh no. No, no, no." Lucia grabbed for the cookbook in Katy's hands, the closet item to use as a physical barrier. Neither Katy nor Lily spoke another word. In fact, they turned toward the supplies, but their lingering smirks said they hadn't let the matter go.

Lucia read the cookbook's introduction, shutting out the other two women. For now, she would focus on baking. *The Electric Co.?* She'd never used a cookbook before ... what was this, *degree?* Four hundred and twenty-five of them sounded really warm. Was that how hot a fire got? She'd never thought about it, just knew exactly what adjustments to make to cause the oven to bake as she needed it to. Their apartment had electric light but not an electric oven. Mamma Vella could likely feed the whole city with an electric oven.

Leaving the book open to the sugar cookie recipe, Lucia offered to mix while Lily and Katy measured the ingredients. The easy camaraderie between the two friends eased some of Lucia's worry, but she found her thoughts lingering on Gio. Why couldn't she forget about him? Even if he cared for her more specially than any other woman, he obviously wasn't in a place to do anything about it. For her heart's sake, Lucia needed to let him go. If only her loneliness didn't vanish whenever he was around.

"There's my favorite girl." Miles entered the room, somehow silent on his feet for such a large man. He pressed a kiss to Lily's cheek, and the woman turned pink. Then he gave Katy a grin before settling his intense gaze on Lucia. "I am glad you decided to join these two. How are you?"

Unnerved, Lucia took a step back.

"Miles, you're scaring her." Lily took the bowl from Lucia's hands. "Don't mind him. I thought Miles a bear at first, but he's really all sweet."

"You'll spoil my reputation." Miles rubbed his ear. "Truly, though, won't you join me in the parlor, Lucia?"

Lucia glanced from Lily to Miles, unsure about the situation. But Lily pushed Lucia toward Miles, who held open the kitchen door before leading her down the hallway to the room just off the front entry. How Mrs. St. Thomas kept her cluttered shelves so free of dust was a marvel. She fingered an intricately woven doily that hung across the back of a chair.

Miles's hand covered her shoulder. "You can be honest with me. Are you doing all right?"

She turned to face him and Miles bent to put himself on eye level. Somehow it shrank him so that he didn't feel so intimidating. "I'll be okay."

Miles frowned, then waved her toward the chair with the doily. "Sit with me a moment?"

Lucia perched on the edge of her seat, weaving her fingers together to keep them still as she watched Miles lower himself to a couch. His large frame looked ill-at-ease on the floral fabric. It nearly made her smile, until she remembered that Miles was Gio's closest friend. Did he approve of her? Did he plan to interrogate her? But she hadn't done anything wrong.

"How much do you know about Gio?" Miles interrupted her thoughts before they careened away from her.

A good question. How much did she really know? Not enough. Not about his past, nor about why he was guarded. But what would Miles think of her if she admitted she'd taken off to another state with a man who was little more than a passing acquaintance—observed, admired, but mostly from afar? No. Better to answer by addressing what everyone seemed to think they knew. "Why does everyone assume he and I—"

Miles held up a large hand. "I have known Gio a long time. Yet he has not shared much with me either."

Really?

"However, he has been there for me during my hardest days. Days of loss and danger. Days when my faith was not as strong as I needed it to be. It is time for me to return that favor. Whatever you need, Lucia, please tell me. Security is what I do, so you are in safe hands. Gio will return with answers, and we can develop a plan to get you home to your grandfather. Okay?"

Lucia nodded, taken aback by Miles's kindness.

"When he returns, ask Gio why he gave you his St. Christopher."

Lucia startled.

Miles rested his elbows on his knees. "I've only known him to part with it one other time. The fact he did so without explanation ... Be patient with him."

Questions pounded Lucia's head like hailstones. "I don't understand. Why would I need to be patient with him?"

"I apologize." Miles smiled. "What you say is true, that everyone makes assumptions about the two of you. I know Gio well enough to know the confusion is not because of you, but because of him. He treats you as one would someone special, such as giving you his St. Christopher."

"But he is kind to everyone." Only, Miles was right. She uncrossed her legs and sat forward. "You know I asked him why he brought me here, why it seems he sees me differently, and you know what he did? He denied it and ran back to Chicago." She pressed her lips together to stop the words of frustration and hurt that wanted to pour out.

"Lucia, then the only person he's lying to is himself." Miles held her gaze with an intensity that Lucia wanted to escape but couldn't. "He might be like a brother to me, but that only means I'm willing to confront him when needed. Like he does for me. If you need an ally, Lucia, you come to me. I refuse to stand by and say nothing if he's only going to break your heart. Do you understand?"

Lucia's jaw fell open, and a sense of security wrapped around her.

"Lucia, wait until you see this oven!" Lily peeked into the room. "Did I miss something?"

Miles's smile chased away his intensity. "Simply welcoming Lucia into the family."

Lily leaned against the arm of Lucia's chair. "He didn't scare you away? I won't let him."

Miles looked up at his girl. "I told her she should ask Gio about his St. Christopher."

Lucia glanced between them. "Why do you both seem to know more about it than anyone else? I didn't even know he carried one."

"Gio gave it to me during the worst of my trial a few weeks ago." Lily fingered the place it must have hung around her neck. The same place Gio always rubbed on his own chest.

The questions pounded harder, aiming for Lucia's heart this time. Why had he given Lily something that obviously meant a good bit to him? Why had he given the same pendent to Lucia? Why had he left her without an explanation?

Gio turned up the collar on his coat as he trudged past the locked-up buildings that had been rapidly built for the World's Fair that opened this past spring. The public's response to the exhibition had been so positive, it would reopen in '34. Now, however, the buildings sat quietly in the dusky light, waiting out the harsh winter. A Century of Progress. Hard to see when half of the city was out of work.

Lake Michigan slopped waves up against the shoreline as Gio left Leif Erickson Drive to slip past the General Motors building and down to the 31st Boat Landing.

"I don't like meeting here." Jan Varga glared at Gio as he approached. A gray scarf hid half of his pockmarked face and his cap sat low over his eyes. "There's no easy escape if someone catches us here."

"Then make it fast." Gio shoved his freezing hands into his pockets, not daring to turn away from the man despite the frozen spray splashing his face. "What news of Lucia Critelli do you have for me?"

"Ettore is actively searching for her. Nor has he taken another mistress, girlfriend, or whatever. He's been asking about you, too, after he learned her grandfather is staying with your family. Care to tell me why?"

Gio shrugged. "I help people. She disappeared. Her grandfather is my neighbor. I help him."

Jan narrowed his sharp, blue eyes. "You are not hiding her?"

Gio looked toward heaven, praying he would come across as authentic in his rebuttal. "If I hide her, why would I also look for her?"

Jan sidled closer and lowered his voice. "Why do you want to find her?"

"Her grandfather, he is worried and this is what I do. Do you have any more information for me?" He pulled a coin from his pocket, rolling it through stiff fingers to loosen Jan's tongue.

"No one else cares about the woman, only Ettore and you. He is also willing to hire eyes and ears."

Like Jan, no doubt, which meant Gio needed to tread carefully.

"My payment?" Jan wiggled his fingers.

Gio held it just out of reach. "Why does he care? What is she to him?"

Jan squinted at him. "You care about this girl more than the others."

Gio forced a snort and slammed the coin into Jan's waiting hand. "She is unmarried. If I care about her more than others, why have I not married her?" The question jarred Gio's conscience.

"The Matchmaker would know." Jan winked, pocketed the coin, and turned on his heel, then stopped and lowered his scarf. "Say ... how *would* one go about asking a girl—never mind."

"Asking her for a date? Or for marriage?" Gio hid his smile at Jan's sudden change into awkwardness.

"We have gone on dates. I want to ... not marry, but, uh, go steady."

Gio clapped the man on the shoulder. "Her favorite activity, what is it?"

"She wants to see *Little Women* at the movies." Jan didn't hide his disgust. "Though, I suppose Hepburn is pretty enough."

"Do not say that to her." Gio refrained from shaking his head. "Take her to see this *Little Women* because it will make her happy."

"What about me enjoying it?"

"You like to see her happy?"

"Well, yeah."

Gio shrugged, but his own question burrowed into his mind, right beside the one about marrying Lucia. Gio ignored both as he led the way back toward the bustling streets. "She like flowers?"

"Yes."

"Do not forget those."

"Who has money for this?"

Gio nodded toward the pocket where Jan had stuffed the coin.

Red rose on Jan's chapped cheeks.

Gio said no more and disappeared into the crowd. A backward glance, however, showed another man stepping from the shadows to follow him. Gio sighed. He'd have to go about his normal day before searching for more information about Lucia.

Supper could not come soon enough.

"Giosuè!" Mamma rushed him as he pushed into the quiet house. Any moment his brothers would return from work, their wives from offering aid, and the young ones from playing in the neighborhood. The warmth from the oven—and Mamma's all-encompassing hug—thawed him like the snowflakes that melted when they hit the street.

"I am well, Mamma." Gio laughed as she kissed his cheeks, then hugged him again. "I left the house only an hour ago."

"The streets are dangerous, especially at this time of day." Mamma replied in Italian, waving the wooden spoon she held in one hand. "With Lucia disappearing ... from church of all places—is nowhere safe? You come sit before the others get home. I made soup and bread and that bird you brought home. A pheasant was it? Where did you get such a thing?"

"I find things, Mamma." Gio sat at the table, nodding at Ugo, who sipped his coffee across from him. "Are you well?" he asked the older man, continuing in Italian. Ugo had been abed when Gio dropped off his belongings upon his arrival in town that afternoon.

"As well as I can be when my Lucia is in hiding. Why can you not marry her, my boy? I know she loves you. I know you care for her. It would make this old heart happy. It would protect her from the likes of Emberto Ettore. Why will you not do this?"

A physical knife would hurt less. "I cannot marry her. I am not fit to be her husband." *If I care about her more than others, why have I not married her? You like to see her happy?*

Mamma scoffed as she set a cup of coffee and plate of cookies before him. "You will be a good husband and she a good wife."

"I agree, she will be a wonderful wife." Gio couldn't add that it should be to someone else—couldn't bear to picture such a thing. Lucia had been right to ask him why he had not played matchmaker for her. "We care for each other as friends. Nothing more. Will both of you please leave it at that?"

"Fine. Then when can my Lucia return home?" Coffee sloshed as Ugo set the cup on the table. Mamma had the spill cleaned up in an instant.

"Not as soon as I hoped." Gio schooled his tone, shoving the previous topic beside the questions that jabbed at him. "Ettore is still searching for her."

"Why?" Ugo moaned. "Why must she face this?"

"Why, indeed." Mamma tasted the soup bubbling in the pot on the stove. "A sweet girl like Lucia. Why would that goon do something as horrible as take her?"

Her and other women. The thought soured Gio's stomach. He wasn't naive to think this was the first time Ettore had done this, nor was he the only one to traffic women. Because of the Volstead Act, most people focused on the illegal sale of alcohol, on which Al Capone cornered the Chicago market back in '29 when he massacred Moran's men.

Gio hid a shudder. He still remembered the sounds of sirens from that awful day.

But alcohol was only the beginning. Gambling and prostitution went along with the illegal sale of alcohol. And with the pipelines easily bringing the alcohol down from Canada through the porous state of Wisconsin, what else had they been able to move?

Now, with the sale of alcohol legal again, they would be anxious to replace their revenue stream. Add to that, numerous men without work. Families losing their homes. Immigrants getting the last and lowest jobs available. And women losing the work they gained during the Great War to men, leaving the women with no means of support unless they had a husband or father who had a job. What did that do for someone like Lucia? Gio stared into the soup his mamma set before him. The picture it created, the future it formed, seemed incredibly bleak.

Softly, like a whisper on the wind, the words to Christina Rossetti's poem *In the Bleak Midwinter* crossed his mind. He'd first heard it in a Methodist church he delivered food to, and it had stuck with him.

What can I give Him, Poor as I am?

What, indeed? Gio lowered his head, as if to pray over his soup, then closed his eyes, his prayer in his native tongue.

God, I give you my hands, my feet, my heart. Help me spread your goodwill to all I meet. And Lucia ... Gio's words failed. He never struggled with prayer, with talking to his Heavenly Father. But now, with her? He still had no idea what to pray.

Chapter 6

Saturday, December 9

Gio arrived back in Eagle on Saturday afternoon. Miles had told him about the Christmas pageant occurring that night, and the closer it came, the more Gio couldn't deny how much he wanted to make it back in time to attend. Why? Because he missed Lucia.

At first, he'd planned to ignore or fight that feeling by purposefully avoiding the Christmas pageant. But watching the couples strolling along Michigan Avenue, listening to his own brothers talk about their families, and fielding the questions from Lucia's anxious grandfather ... it was all too much for him.

It certainly didn't help that he worried for her safety. While Ettore remained in Chicago, he was searching for Lucia. Gio had to make himself scarce to avoid being questioned. Why Ettore still wanted to find Lucia, Gio could not gather. It seemed no one knew why the man hadn't just moved on to another woman, another Italian woman if that's what he wanted.

Gio planned to find the answer, even if it meant interrogating Ettore himself, but Saturday had come around too quickly, and Gio returned to Eagle with an hour to spare before the program.

"You need a suit." Miles adjusted his tie in the small mirror on the wall of his rented room in Mrs. St. Thomas's boarding house.

"I have one, mio amico." Gio tossed his newsboy cap on the bed. "Mrs. St. Thomas had a room open next door to yours. I put my knapsack there."

"Then why are you in here?" Miles made eye contact through the mirror. "It wouldn't happen to have anything to do with a certain Italian signorina, would it?"

Gio sank onto the bed.

"Wow. I remember feeling like you look. Is the danger that bad, or have you fallen head over heels?"

"Both." He could confess it to his friend, right?

"I'm glad you finally admitted it." Miles buttoned his vest. "Even Lucia knows you think of her differently than any other woman. You going to tell her the truth?"

"No." He wouldn't tell Lucia. Couldn't. Because then he'd have to tell her why nothing could come of these feelings.

Miles crossed his arms. "I don't approve."

"It is none of your ... *affari.* Your ..." Gio growled.

"Business. I know. Fine. What is the danger level she faces?"

Gio dragged his thoughts away from his disgust with himself—how unfair he was being to Lucia, how much he'd end up hurting her despite his best efforts, how he wished overcoming his past was as easy as finding ... anything.

"Gio?" Miles stood over him, and Gio pushed to his feet, away from his friend, but Miles's words chased him as he headed for the door. "You're never this distracted. What's really going on?"

Gio spun, his stomach sour with regret. "It is easier to stay away from her when there is no danger. Now? I must confront what I have hidden in my heart. I am man enough to admit I do not want to see her married to someone else. But I cannot marry her. I will not."

"Why?" The softness of the question coming from his large friend caused Gio to lean into the wall, his knees weakened.

Unexpected tears he buried long ago pressed against his eyes but he fought them back with a mask of irritation. "That is not the issue. I will not allow myself to become distracted, you may trust me on that. Ettore is dangerous. He is not looking for a *padrona* or mistress, or he would forget Lucia. There must be another reason Ettore wants her."

"Okay." Miles drew out the word. "Do you know why?"

"I do not." Gio rested his chin on his chest. All his abilities at finding answers and to this one question, he failed.

"Have you asked Lucia?"

"Interrogate her as I would one of Ettore's goons? Mio amico, I cannot."

Miles suddenly stood before him, the intimidating soldier. "You need to make peace with your past, amico, it's obstructing your comprehension. I'm not suggesting you interrogate Lucia. If you do, you answer to me. Understand?"

Gio swallowed. He never planned to revisit the reason he chose never to marry, but if it meant Lucia's safety, he must.

"Start by being honest with her." Miles threaded his arms into his suit jacket. "Then tell her why you need answers. She wants out of this mess as much as you desire to help her. And she cares about you."

"The table, it has turned, has it not?" Gio offered a tired smile to his friend. "Who was I to offer you advice?"

"You were—and still are—my friend." Miles clapped his shoulder. "And now I return the favor. I couldn't have saved Lily without you."

A rainy-snowy mix spit from the sky as Gio walked to the church, alone. Miles had already left to drive Lily, and Joey would bring Katy and Lucia. Gio blew into cupped hands before rubbing them together. Would Lucia be glad to see him? Would having no answers help or hurt his chances? Why did it matter if he couldn't act on these feelings?

Like a ghost from Christmas Past, the question that had dogged him since he'd watched the pine casket of the woman he once loved lowered into the ground ... even now it whispered in his ear: could he ever do enough?

Lucia spotted Gio before he saw her—or, at least, acknowledged her. Joey and Katy slipped inside the church, and Lucia waited at the corner for him to reach her.

"Gio?"

Surprise showed on his face. He hadn't seen her. "Lucia, why are you not inside? It is cold and not safe for you to be alone."

"I'm not alone, am I?" Lucia didn't mean to sound flirty, but between being inordinately happy to see him and the desire to lift what appeared to be his despairing mood, the tone tumbled right out with her words. Her cheeks heated and she lowered her chin.

"No. You are not alone." Gio wove her hand around his arm. "May I escort you to the *programma natalizio*, Signorina Critelli?"

Lucia hid a smile at his formal request and nodded. "I didn't expect you back so soon. Does that mean it is safe for me to return to Nonno?"

"No. Not yet. We speak after?"

Lucia had little choice but to agree as they reached the church doors. While Gio's words churned her worry, how could fear flourish when surrounded by Christmas?

Evergreen boughs decorated the sills of the beautiful stained glass windows, filling the air with their cozy aroma. Candles burned on the altar. The priest—*pastor*, for this was not a Catholic church as Lucia was used to attending—welcomed the congregation as children filed onto the raised area that held his pulpit.

Lucia's heart puddled as the little voices sang, "Angels We Have Heard on High." The "gloria" part was about as not-together as it could possibly be, but the children belted out the notes. Beside her, Gio's shoulders vibrated with a silent chuckle and she fought hard not to join him.

The children sang two more Christmas hymns before a trio of young women lent their voices to "O Little Town of Bethlehem" and a quartet of young men rendered an unusually up-tempo version of "We Three Kings," about which Gio whispered in Italian that the camels in this particular rendition seemed to be traveling *rapido*.

The highlight of the evening, however, were the last few songs, which the entire congregation was invited to sing. Lucia's heart swelled full-to-bursting as she sang, but at the initial stanzas of "Silent Night," she fell silent. Beside her, almost in a whisper, Gio sang for the first time that night.

Notte silenziosa, notte Santa ...

Tears pricked Lucia's eyes. Not just at the incredible voice she didn't realize Gio had, but at how holy the moment felt. Around her, people she didn't know raised their voices together. Young and old. Rich and poor. Farmers and city dwellers. American and Irish and Italian. It mattered not. All of them had one wish for this Christmas season ...

... Dormi nella pace divina ... to sleep in heavenly peace.

Would her peace return? Would her world right itself? Would she be able to spend Christmas with Nonno? Lucia glanced at the man beside her. Would there be a future for them?

The pastor offered a prayer and a benediction, then the congregation filed into a large room with tables filled with Christmas goodies. Lucia easily spotted the cookies she'd helped Lily and Katy bake—amazing what one could do with an electric oven! There were several other varieties, plus cake of varying kinds, and even punch.

Good cheer seemed to permeate the room, but Lucia struggled to let it pull her from her contemplations. Listening to Gio sing had nestled in her soul like a seed, and she wanted to let those thoughts germinate.

"Need air?" Gio's voice whispered in her ear.

She nodded and let him lead her outside. The precipitation had turned fully to snow since they'd entered the church, and now a light layer of white lay across the gravestones in the cemetery. Wreaths hung over many of them, showing how much family members still missed those interred there.

"Let us walk along the street." Gio turned her away from the cemetery.

"Is there a reason you don't wish to walk there?" She nodded toward the gravestones. She would have loved to get a closer look at the statue in the center of the graveyard. "There is a bench there."

"No." A strangely serious expression clouded Gio's features, but he said no more.

"Can you tell me about Chicago? Why can't I go home yet? I hate spending Christmas away from Nonno."

"I understand, Lucia. I do. Ettore, he still searches for you. I do not know why." Gio stopped and took her hands in his.

The gesture surely wasn't meant to be romantic, but how could it not be? The snow softly falling around them. The quiet of the evening. The remnants of the Christmas music wafting in the air. Heavens. She was hopeless when it came to her feelings for this man. Would she ever be able to let him go? He refused to see her as more than a friend. That wasn't enough for her, which meant she needed to end whatever this was between them before the hurt it would cause became too much for either of them to manage.

"Ettore, why did he coerce you?"

Lucia straightened, and the intensity of Gio's look had her stepping back, though he didn't release her hands.

So much for her romantic thoughts. Her ears pounded. This was good. Right? Focus on the problem. Not on the romance.

"Lucia."

"He wanted me to deliver something," The memory played like a silent film before her eyes and caused her words to pour out hot and defensive. "He needed a messenger. That's what he said. A messenger or delivery or something like that."

"What did he want delivered?" The sharpness in Gio's tone sliced through the memory, pulling Lucia back to the snowy sidewalk. "Tell me you weren't the delivery."

"He ... he never told me." Nausea turned her stomach. Why had Gio pulled her from a Christmas service out into a magical snowscape to ask her about those awful hours? "He spent the morning delivering those kidnapped girls to who-knows-where. Gio, we have to stop him. He cannot continue to hurt those women. We have to do something."

I have to do something.

"I know." Gio's softened voice and gentle touch made her realize she clung to him as if he were her valiant knight. He was a knight, just not hers. "We will help them. Later."

"No." Lucia wrenched her hands away as the heartache she'd hoped to save herself from bloomed in her chest. "That is not good enough, Gio. Do not put me off. I hate hiding when there's something I can do to help those girls. Let me go to the police—I'll testify."

"No." Gio slashed the air with his hands. "My brothers, they know. That is enough."

"It's not. To stop Ettore, secondhand details will never do."

Gio muttered something in Italian, then stayed in his native tongue as he said, "You know what happens to witnesses who testify against men like Emberto Ettore. I will not let you become a victim to his violence."

"I already am, Gio." The Italian words flowed easily thanks to the pain churning her stomach. "We need to stop him. I don't care what it takes. Those women deserve someone who is willing to take down the monster who is kidnapping them. I know he's only one person. I know there are others. But we have to start somewhere."

"Then tell me—" Gio grabbed her shoulders— "what was special about you that he singled you out?"

"Oh Gio, I am not special." If anyone knew that, she did and it took the fight right out of her. Wasn't Gio's very resistance to her proof? "There is no reason. Nothing."

"A man like Ettore always has a reason."

A tear squeezed from the corner of her eye. "Maybe I was accessible? He needed someone, so he chose me. He had been keeping an eye on me for a couple weeks." Lucia shuddered.

Gio tugged her into his arms. "Why did you go with him so easily? Why not put up a fight?"

"He threatened Nonno. I would do anything to protect him—you know that." Lucia pulled away the slightest bit. "I left you my bag. Did you not find it? Or why doubt me like this?"

Gio's gaze roved over her face, pausing on her lips before returning to her eyes. "I do not doubt you, Lucia. What's more, I will find answers for you, and I will get you home."

Lucia gulped. During her weakest moments, she'd dreamed about how it would feel to be in Gio's arms, but this? This was much more encompassing than she ever imagined. Her heart banged against her ribs, her mouth went completely dry, and her emotions spun like a compass that had lost due north.

Gio ran his thumb over her cheekbone, then he lowered his mouth to hers. Her knees weakened, but Gio held her. This is what she'd wished for since she first met Gio Vella. This was a dream come true.

He pulled away. "I am sorry. I forgot myself." His voice came out rough ... but firm.

Lucia blinked. "W-what do you mean?"

"I won't kiss a woman I cannot marry."

"I'm not asking for a proposal, Gio. We were talking about my safety."

"More reason. I am sorry. I made a mistake."

A mistake? Lucia gritted her teeth against the sob that wanted to burst from her. "I thought you cared about me. Am I really that foolish of a girl?" When he just stared at her with sorrowful eyes, she took a step back and jerked her chin up. "Obviously, I am. I had a schoolgirl crush. No more. If you want to risk your neck talking to Emberto, then go ahead. I'm returning to Chicago tomorrow, collecting Nonno, then going ... somewhere. A place neither you nor Emberto can find me."

"Lucia."

"Don't, Gio." Lucia slammed her hands in her pockets, hurt and anger and grief washing over her. How could she be so stupid? How could—

In her pocket was a small item. She didn't recall it being there before. Slowly, she withdrew it so that it lay in the palm of her gloved hand. A diamond ring?

"Wait ..." She stared at Gio. "Is this how you planned to propose to me?"

Chapter 7

"**N**o!" Gio's eyes shot open wide, then he reined in his shock at the hurt that shuttered Lucia's expression.

Mamma Mia, how could he have let himself kiss her? If only he could blame it on Ugo and Mamma and Miles for planting ideas in his head. Now he was making everything even worse than his bumbling attempts at questioning her. Questioning Lucia. He owed Miles for that lovely suggestion.

"Then what is this?" Lucia shook what looked like a diamond ring.

He risked a step closer to hold out his hand for it. She slapped it into his palm.

"Take it. Katy will give me a ride to her home. I'll find my own way back to Chicago."

The ring glistened in the gaslight, snowflakes caressing it. The diamond was one of the largest he'd seen. Set in a gold band. How had it come to be in Lucia's pocket?

Then her words penetrated his fog—she was going back to Chicago without him—and he looked up. But Lucia was gone.

He couldn't let her return to Chicago without someone to protect her. He had no doubt Ettore would know the moment she set foot inside the city limits. Gio stuffed the ring deep into his own coat pocket. He'd investigate its origin after he made sure Lucia didn't do something foolish just because Gio was *un stupido*.

Hopefully, he could enlist the help of his friends too. Miles and Joey would side with him on keeping Lucia away from Chicago, but he wasn't sure about Lily. She was an independent woman. And Katy ... would her Irish heritage work against them?

Gio dashed into the church hall just as two furry creatures darted past his legs, nearly knocking his feet out from under him. He caught himself on the punch table, tipping it toward him so that the bowl and cups slid his way. Unable to correct his balance, he let himself crash to the ground, catching the punch bowl as it slid off the table.

Cups clattered and shouts erupted. Gio looked up, expecting the growing chaos to be pointed at him. No. The shouts were about something else entirely. Five dogs ran around the room, jumping up on tables for food, rubbing on people for attention, snuffling around the floor for crumbs. Dogs? That must have been what knocked him over, but how ...

A whistle he wouldn't mistake anywhere split the air. Silence descended, and Lily called the dogs to her side. From his position on the floor, Gio could barely see past pant legs and skirts, but the crowd parted as Lily led the dogs past him, her own two, Pieter and Smokey, in the lead. Were the rest her latest group of trainees?

Miles jogged past him but skidded to a stop. "What happened to you?"

Gio handed him the punch bowl and leapt to his feet. "Dogs. How did they get here?"

Miles scrubbed his beard. The man never could decide whether to be clean shaven or not. "With help."

Gio felt his frown deepening. "The trouble from October, it is over, si?"

"I'll call my contacts to make sure all parties are all still locked up, but this has the same feel as the sabotage Lily faced when I first got to town."

Gio had been thinking the same thing. "I am here to help, mio amico, but *primo*, have you seen Lucia?"

"I haven't." Miles trotted after Lily.

Gio watched his retreating form for a moment, rubbing the spot where the St. Christopher usually hung from his neck. How had he made such a mess of things? For all his good intentions, he was no better than the lovesick fool he'd been when he left for the Great War. Not only had he not learned his lesson, apparently, his actions could once again cost a woman her life.

"Which way did they go?" Joey broke into Gio's thoughts as he hurried up, Katy's hand tightly in his. "I need to get the chief to meet us at the house before they touch anything. Evidence, you know."

Gio pointed his thumb over his shoulder and the two were gone. Lucia no longer had her own ride to Katy's home—surely, she wouldn't take a ride from just any stranger—which meant he could take a moment to breathe before he searched. Then again, perhaps she'd walked back to Katy's. It wasn't as far as they often walked in the city, though it felt much farther here in the country's darkness.

That spurred him into action. He checked outside, even walking through the cemetery and around the block, with no sign of her. He finally returned to the hall, which was now mostly empty. Where hadn't he looked yet?

"Mr. Vella." Mrs. St. Thomas smiled at him. She loved Miles, and any friend of Miles was a friend of hers—at least, that's what she'd told him when he'd asked if she had a room for him. "You appear lost."

"Have you seen Lucia—er Signorina Critelli?"

Mrs. St. Thomas pressed a wrinkled hand against her throat. "I haven't. Not after Lily's dogs barreled through here. You know, she's trouble. I tried to warn Miles, but he's smitten with her. A man like him could have—"

"Si, si, Mrs. St. T'omas." Gio grimaced apologetically. He still couldn't say her name without his accent.

The older woman patted his arm. "If I see that sweet young lady, I'll tell her you're looking for her."

"Grazie." Gio smiled. Good thing the woman's feelings about Lily didn't extend toward Lucia. He turned for the door. Maybe he'd find her walking the road to Katy's house.

"Did you check the sanctuary?" Mrs. St. Thomas's words stopped him. Why hadn't he thought of that?

"Grazie *mille*, Signora."

He entered from the rear. The room lay in shadow, with only the soft light of the moon reflecting off the snow and filtering in through the stained glass windows, but Gio immediately spotted the small form sitting in the front pew. His quiet steps echoed in the room, bringing up the person's head. Lucia. He'd found her. A breath of relief left him.

Lucia stood at the end of the aisle as Gio walked toward her. He kept his pace slow, and visions of this scenario—only in reverse—flashed through his mind, church bells ringing, and Lucia in white. The ring in his pocket called to him. She'd thought he'd intended to propose, and his vehement denial had hurt her. Yet if he ever married, Lucia was the only woman he wanted to spend the rest of his life with. He knew that. Felt it deeply. If only he could.

Gio stopped two feet away. Far enough that he wouldn't be tempted to reach for her. Her vulnerability screamed at him, chastised him. She didn't smile, but neither were there tears in her eyes. She only looked at him questioningly. And maybe hopefully? Had this moment, the implications of being here together in the silent church, impacted her as it had him? He must be gentle with her.

"I could not find you." Gio rubbed the St. Christopher's empty place. Despite his intentions, the sentence came out sounding slightly accusatory.

"I've been here the whole time." Lucia whispered the words. Did they have a double meaning?

"*Mi dispiace.*" Oh how sorry he was, for so many things.

Lucia closed the distance, resting her hand on his arm. Perhaps she sensed how deeply his remorse went?

"Forgive me?" He studied her eyes. Brown and beautiful, with a light that always called to him.

"I am sorry, too, Gio. I should not have scolded you or jumped to conclusions." Lucia bowed her head. "I'm scared. And that makes me rash."

Against his better judgment, Gio pulled her into his arms again and rested his chin on her hair. He had no words to help her, could only fumble through a prayer. As he did, he could almost hear the remnants of the Christmas hymns they had sung earlier that evening. The promises of hope, peace, and light that accompanied the celebration of Christmas, the birth of the Christ Child.

"Why did you give me the St. Christopher?" Lucia's thoughts must have gone the same place his had.

Gio tightened his hold on her. "We had nothing when we left Italia. I hated God for it. The tenement in New York City, it was ... worse." Painful memories tumbled through Gio's mind.

Lucia nestled closer, bringing him back to the dark sanctuary.

"Our neighbors, they believed in God. They showed me a new way of trusting Him. I found hope again. When I left for the war, they gave me the medallion. It reminds me of God, of his protection." Gio swallowed. "Will you wear it?"

Lucia pulled away and Gio's heart sank. Then she tugged on a chain around her neck, lifting the St. Christopher from behind the collar of her dress. She wore his gift.

"Ah, mia bella," the whispered words slipped between his lips.

"Gio, do you still trust God that way? The way you did before you left for the war?"

The question hit him in the heart. With the disparity between his first love and Lucia staring him in the face, he wanted to react, to lash out at Lucia for asking him, because he felt the nugget of truth for what it was—conviction. He prayed more than he ever had. He provided spiritual wisdom and guidance for others in as much supply as requested. But when it came to his own life, he continually sought answers he had yet to find.

Lucia closed his hand around the St. Christopher she rested in his palm. "This won't provide me protection."

"I know that." Gio snapped the words. "I didn't offer because it has some magical powers. I want you to remember—" He yanked himself away from her touch. The pain of his former girl's rejection from all those years ago pushed to the surface like a thorn.

Lucia rested light fingers on his shoulder. "Gio, do you want me to remember God's protection ... or yours?"

Gio's breath caught.

Before either could respond, Miles's voice reverberated through the sanctuary. "Gio! Lucia!"

"We're here." Gio shoved the moment away, setting the St. Christopher back into Lucia's hand, and headed for the door where Miles waited. Lucia hurried next to him, but before he realized what she was doing, she'd worked his hand open and slipped the St. Christopher inside.

"We need to convene and make a plan to find whoever released Lily's dogs." Miles stood large, looking like the soldier he was.

A mission. An action Gio could focus on instead of this unsettled searching in his soul. And he'd keep Lucia close so she didn't run away to Chicago without him.

"We will follow, mio amico." But first, Lucia. He'd been a fool and wouldn't repay her forgiveness by walking away. He tugged her to a stop and put the St. Christopher back into her hand for the second time that night. "Keep this safe for me?"

She looked at him with wide eyes, and he knew she grasped his double meaning. He wasn't just giving her the medallion. He was placing his bruised heart in her hands.

Lucia rubbed a thumb over the St. Christopher that rested in her dress pocket as Gio and his friends gradually settled around Lily's kitchen table, each with a mug of hot chocolate. Gio hadn't paid Lucia any attention since he gave her the medallion, other than making sure she joined them.

She would have preferred to retreat to a quiet space to think. Gio's behavior baffled her. One minute she felt as if she were the only woman in his world; the next, he ignored her completely. With no way of returning to Katy's house without someone to take her—perhaps she could have asked Mrs. St. Thomas, but Gio hadn't exactly given Lucia an option—here Lucia sat.

"Someone is attacking Lily's business again, and I want to know who." Miles set down his cup with a bang, sloshing hot chocolate over the rim.

Lucia jumped at the noise and tried to slide farther away from the group without appearing as if she did so. She didn't belong. These were Gio's friends, not hers, and it appeared that Gio cared more for them than her. Why else would he have dropped their conversation at the church—even dropped his investigation into the threat against her—and come running to Lily's rescue? It shouldn't matter so much to her, but it did. She fingered the St. Christopher. If she was nothing more than one of the many women Gio helped, then why give her this?

"Do not worry, mio amico." Gio had a pencil and pad of paper set before him. "We will find answers. Like last time."

"Working together, we can solve this," Joey said.

Lily ran the cuff of her sleeve through her fingers, and Katy's fingers tightened on her mug.

Lucia wished she had something to offer, but she was a stranger here. Lily's dog Smokey must have sensed her discomfort because he curled up on her shoes. From Lucia's vantage point, she had a perfect view to the picture window in the other room. The snow fell, reflecting the ambient light that managed to filter through the night. The peace and stillness cast a blanket of calm over her heart, allowing her to tune back in to the conversation happening around her.

"That's a plan." Miles sat back in his chair, giving a nod to Joey. "I'll take days, you take nights. We'll make sure no one has access to the barn."

"No." Lily shook her head. "Neither of you can spend all your time guarding my barn."

"You going to stop us?" Joey raised his eyebrow.

Lily cast a pleading look at Katy.

"It be a good plan." Katy shrugged.

Lily rolled her eyes. "Fine."

"Now that's settled." Miles turned to Gio. "What's got you all up-tight? Do you have news from Chicago?"

Lucia sat up. He had news and had interrogated her instead of told her?

Gio drew out the ring, holding it between his dark fingers so that it sparkled in the electric light like a star in the night sky. Gasps echoed around the room before all eyes fell on Lucia.

"Did you propose?" Lily's hissed whisper easily reached Lucia, caus-ing heat to shoot up Lucia's neck.

"No." Gio's eyes didn't leave the ring. "This is why Lucia is here. Ettore, he put it in her pocket."

"You did not know?" Katy turned wide eyes on Lucia.

"No." Lucia spoke defensively, even though she detected no accu-sation. "I don't know when or how it got into my pocket."

"I do." Gio set the ring on the table. "This is why Ettore has not been caught. He hides his packages on girls, and he sends them as his messengers. Ettore wished Lucia deliver this."

"Where were you being sent?" Miles looked at Lucia, the question eerily similar to Gio's interrogation.

"I wasn't being sent anywhere." Lucia folded her arms, the memory of those moments fresh in her mind. "Emberto was taking me somewhere."

Miles's eyebrows rose, and he shared a glance with both Joey and Gio before he spoke. "He was delivering the ring himself and using you as a cover, then, which means he knows you still have it. He won't let you go without getting it back."

Cold replaced the heat. "Why? Why did he choose me? There were other girls in that warehouse." Not that she wanted him to use them either. Lucia bowed her head. How selfish was she? She should be glad Ettore chose her if it saved one of the other girls.

"Lucia?" The softness in Gio's voice made her raise her eyes to his. The awkwardness between them evaporated with the look he gave her. His eyes filled with such compassion that it melted away the barriers she thought she'd built since their time in the church. Heavens, she trusted this man, there was no doubt about that.

"We need to take it back to him." Lucia raised her chin, determined to put an end to their dilemma and save her heart more pain by setting Gio free of her. Then she'd work at saving the other women Ettore planned to use in his schemes. "Let's leave for Chicago tomorrow."

Chapter 8

E mberto Ettore smoothed the lapel of his suit jacket as he strode into the warehouse office.

What had been an illegal smuggling opportunity a week ago was now, thanks to the latest amendment, an open market. And the powers that be were scrambling to adjust to the changes. Of course, that's why he sold his skills to whomever paid. There was job security in that. If only this job hadn't gone sideways.

Two goons stood on either side of the office door. He felt their scrutiny, even while they didn't appear to watch him approach.

"He wanted to see me." Emberto held his arms out as the goon on the right stepped forward to pat him down. He had no choice but to relinquish his weapons, adding to his unease. He cloaked it with a condescending sneer.

"Boss said to go in." The goon on the left nodded his chin toward the door as if Emberto was no more than an inconvenient paperboy delivering unwelcome news.

Emberto refused to let it rattle him and took a fortifying breath.

"Sit." The scrawny, middle-aged man behind the desk pointed to the open chair across from him. Then he folded bony fingers and rested pointy elbows on the papers littering the desktop as he leaned forward. "I expected delivery a week ago."

"Moving the package did not go as planned." Emberto went with veiled honesty. "I am working to correct the problem."

"You are a middle man with double loyalties." Signore Gennaro glanced toward the gun that lay beside his elbow. "I have no need of you."

"I know who has the ring." Emberto grimaced at the desperation in his voice.

Gennaro raised gray eyebrows.

"The heat from—" Emberto cut himself off. Men like Gennaro hated excuses. "As usual, I planned to use a girl to deliver the package, as a bonus gift to you. I couldn't use one of my usual runners." Because both the Feds and Touhy's goons were sniffing around Ice Connor's death.

"And this runner, she took the ring." Statement, not question.

"She doesn't know she has it." He hoped.

He'd slipped it into the pocket of her old coat before putting that ridiculous fur coat over top of it. He'd chosen her because he felt confident Lucia Critelli had no clue he had used her as a runner, and in return, no one would guess a sweet, church-going girl like her carried hot merchandise like the ring stolen from the mail truck in Charlotte. It'd been going so well until Giosuè Vella got involved.

Emberto opened his mouth to tell Gennaro about Vella's involvement, then thought better of it. Vella was too protected in this city and garnered too much loyalty.

"I will give you until Christmas Eve to take care of the problem." Gennaro sat back, signifying that the meeting was over. "If you can't deliver as promised ..."

Emberto made his escape, the biting wind that wove through the downtown buildings chasing him as surely as Gennaro's threat. He had to find out where Vella hid the girl. Every one of his sources said Vella hadn't done anything more than take her away from Emberto—something Gennaro would know as well—but Emberto couldn't believe it was as simple as that. Lucia might be sweet, but she was too gullible to hide from Emberto without help. Vella's help. Why else would Vella harbor her grandfather?

Sure, even Emberto's enemies would agree that Giosuè Vella was like the Good Samaritan the Bible thumpers preached about, taking in enemies and binding their wounds. How many times had Vella stopped to help an injured runner? Then again, he'd just as soon allow his Fed brother to arrest one of them. Vella had no ties. No loyalties, except to the poor he helped. The innocent. Emberto spat in the street. Giosuè Vella wasted his talents! What Emberto could do with a man like Vella on his payroll.

He turned into the wind, heading due east. He had no time to spend on Vella's misplaced choices. Emberto needed to find Lucia, needed to find the ring. His life depended on it. He'd start with the grandfather. If that led nowhere, he'd find leverage to use against Vella—a dangerous proposition considering the appreciation he received across the city—but Emberto didn't arrive at his current status by being gun-shy. He took risks. Made deliveries. Executed hits. Did whatever he was hired to do. He hadn't failed yet and he wouldn't now.

Oh yes, he'd find Lucia Critelli, then he'd take her and the ring to Gennaro. Before Christmas Eve.

Chapter 9

Wednesday, December 13

Lucia held her hand out to Glenn the donkey. The afternoon sun failed to warm the air outside, but here in the barn, it was cozy warm. A moment ago, Katy finished mucking the stalls, so now only the smell of hay tickled Lucia's cold nose

It had been four days since Gio left for Chicago. Without her. And without the ring. Not even Miles and Joey knew where Gio had hidden it. Why did these men—albeit large, strong, confident men—insist on making decisions about her life and safety? She'd been on her own, taking care of Nonno, for years. Why couldn't she do so now?

On the other hand, she understood their reasoning. If she didn't have the ring in her possession or knowledge of its whereabouts, no one could hurt her to get it. She'd argued that the knowledge could save her, give her leverage when Ettore found her. But Gio insisted that her leverage was him. He had the ring and wouldn't give up its location if anyone hurt her. Lucia didn't like that any better. Gio hadn't left her a choice.

Meanwhile, Gio was scouting not only the original owner of the ring, but whether it was safe for her to return home. Or, at the very least, how to return the ring to the proper owner without getting them all killed. Miles and Joey had complete faith he'd come through. Lucia was simply weary.

"How did I get in this predicament, Glenn?" She rubbed the donkey's nose. "I hear you protect the barnyard. Does that mean you'll protect me too? I sure do prefer your company to that of any of those other men."

Not that she didn't like them. It was just ... Miles was too intimidating. Joey too intense. And Gio? Well, Gio was destined to break her heart.

"Si, si, Glenn. It is better to be here with you. But I do miss my nonno." Sharp sorrow sliced through her like a bullet. "Did you know, today is the only day Nonno would ever step foot inside the kitchen? He can't cook for anything. But bake ... Glenn, if you could only taste his Santa Lucia Day cookies. The cardamom and ginger." She kissed her fingers and laughed, joy soothing the aching in her soul.

"That sounds like a right fine memory." Katy appeared beside her. "Me grandfather couldn't bake either."

"Is he ..." Lucia stopped, unsure whether to ask if the man was still living. If he was, then he was likely still in the Old Country, far from here. Huh. In Chicago, the Irish and Italians were enemies, but they really had a whole lot in common, like taking refuge in a country not their own.

Katy shook her head. "My grandfather passed on when I was young. But never mind me. Tell me, what is this Santa Lucia Day you were speaking to Glenn about?"

Glenn brayed and kicked at his stall.

"Her life was not all that pleasant." In fact, Lucia struggled with the saint's story because of her connection with it, but Nonno had this way of focusing on the good parts. "We Italians remember her on this day because this is the day she was martyred."

"Och, that is horrible. And you share her name?" Of course, Katy noticed the connection.

"We are often named for the feast day on which we were born or baptized." Lucia shrugged. Would Katy consider the simple explanation sufficient? The concept of telling an Irishwoman about the insecurity she felt sharing a festival day with Santa Lucia left sweat beading on her mittened palms. Her scalp itched beneath her stocking cap. Glenn must have noticed her feelings because he moved with agitation in his stall.

"Then today is the day of your birth?" Katy asked.

"Si, si." Lucia sighed and turned back to Glenn, the ache in her heart pressing tears to her eyes. She'd never spent this day without Nonno. He had this way of making her feel like the light of his eyes. Eyes her patron saint lost all those centuries ago. Lucia shuddered.

"Then we must celebrate. What will make this day special for you?"

Lucia looked to see Katy's expression, discerning only sincerity. Where she would expect hate, there was only compassion. It sparked those tears to slip down her cheeks. That someone who should despise her not only welcomed her into her home, but was willing to bring happiness to a difficult day ... it warmed her like a cup of coffee.

"Lucia?" The gravelly male voice spoke hesitantly from the doorway.

Katy spun, Glenn brayed, and Lucia shook her head. That voice couldn't be here, couldn't be real.

"*Nipotina?*" The gravelly voice came again. *Granddaughter.* Only one person called her that.

"Nonno?" Lucia blinked. How was he standing like a silhouette in the barn doorway? Had she conjured him in her sorrow?

"*Vieni qui.*" *Come here.* He held out his hands, and Lucia flew toward him. Oh yes, he was so very real. He wrapped her in a hug with arms like wiry ropes, surprisingly tight. His words flowed over her like a cordial. How she'd missed this man who had raised her.

"Ya did good, Mr. Vella." Katy's statement lifted Lucia's head from Nonno's chest.

"Si, si." Nonno nodded his square chin toward the man leaning against the inside wall of the barn.

Lucia didn't think. She launched herself at him next, squeezing his neck as tears slipped down her cheeks. How could she ever thank him enough?

Gio always found a certain satisfaction when one of his deliveries brought joy to the recipient. Watching Lucia's reaction to her grandfather, however, hit Gio even deeper. He knew today was her birthday, and he knew how much both she and her grandfather needed to be together today of all days.

But to have Lucia in his arms? Her own clinging to his neck, leaving him no choice but to embrace her? It should have been *his* birthday! The surprise of her action alone could have knocked him over. As it was, had the wall not been behind him, he would have stumbled when she collided with him.

"Grazie, Gio, grazie, grazie. Thank you, thank you for bringing him." Her words whispered against his ear.

Her cheek pressed against his and her tears left a damp trail on his skin. Even with Ugo and Katy looking on, Gio couldn't help holding her tighter. His heart pounded against his ribs. How could he have come to care for this woman as much as he did? How could he continue to do so and not hurt them both?

He swallowed the lump in his throat and lowered his face into her neck. Her black curls, the ones that escaped her hat, brushed his forehead. He had to find a way to be free of his past because he wanted to repeat this greeting. Many times over, for days and years, he wanted to bring her everything her heart desired so it overflowed with joy.

"Ahem." Miles's throat-clearing forced Gio to put space between him and Lucia.

"No, no." Ugo's hands moved in a circle as if trying to get something moving. "*Non fermati.*"

Heat shot through Gio. "Ugo," he growled.

"*Che?*" All innocence, he was—this grandfather who wanted him to *not stop* holding his granddaughter against all propriety, all reason.

"Ugo!" Gio darted his gaze toward Lucia. He wouldn't embarrass her, even as he wished he could comply.

"Don't mind him." Lucia chuckled as she gave her grandfather a doting smile. "This time of year, he is especially wishful that I find a husband, but on this particular day, he always wishes I find an exceptionally good one."

Gio attempted to tamp down the heat that raced through him at Lucia's insinuation. Him, a good husband? No, no. He would not be one of those. But Ugo thought he would be. Did Lucia think so too? Then he spotted the confused expressions of their friends, so Gio quickly explained that St. Lucia, Lucia's patron saint, was killed after refusing to marry, and it was possible her suitor was the one to kill her.

"Och," Katy spluttered. "Then this day she should be celebrated for remaining unmarried."

"It's okay." Lucia looked at everyone in the room as if attempting to calm an encircling pride of lions. "Tell me what you learned about Ettore and the ring. What do we do next?"

That changed the subject, all right. Gio exchanged a look with Miles. His first stop after returning to Eagle with Ugo had been to find Miles and fill him in. Maybe he should have come to Katy's first, but Miles was the tactical specialist. Gio merely delivered messages, made scouting reports, and found things. Necessary, but not helpful when it came to protecting someone he cared about.

"Right." Katy sighed. "Go inside, all of ya. Coffee be on the stove. I have to be finishing chores in the barn."

Lucia drew a breath and rounded her lips to speak, but Gio ushered her out of the barn before he gave in and kissed her. Si, si, a kiss. Gio shoved the desire away. It would only blind him and confuse her.

Once he had her settled around Katy's wooden table with Miles and Ugo, Gio cast Miles an apologetic smile before continuing in Italian. Miles wouldn't understand his words, but none of this information was new to him, and Ugo spoke so little English, he didn't want the older man to feel left out.

"Ettore attempted to pay your grandfather a visit," Gio explained to Lucia. "My brothers deterred him—"

Ugo muttered just what he thought of Ettore, and it wasn't flattering.

"—but I knew it would only be a matter of time before he succeeded." Gio cast Lucia a hesitant smile. "That's one of the main reasons I brought him here. Besides your birthday."

She didn't thank him this time. "Won't Emberto know where to find me, then? Isn't that why we left Nonno in Chicago?"

Gio rubbed his chest. "I left him enough breadcrumbs, I hope he'll find us in a matter of days."

"What?" Lucia looked from him to Ugo to Miles.

Gio captured her hand. "I want this over, Lucia. We need to end this on our terms, not his. I learned Ettore was using you to deliver the ring to a man by the name of Gennaro. Have you heard of him?"

Lucia shook her head.

"He's a higher-up member of one of the Italian crime families. Somewhat friendly with Touhy. That was the connection I needed to piece together the rest. When Capone attempted to frame Touhy, Touhy sent his goons to Charlotte to throw over a mail truck for his bail money. Turns out, the detective they put on the case solved the crime in a matter of weeks, only to find one of the four culprits was dead. A Charles 'Ice' Connors."

"Ettore, wasn't it?" Ugo asked, arms folded against his chest.

Gio gave a noncommittal shrug. He talked to enough people to suspect it was true, but everyone knew not to admit to actually knowing it. "With the heat from the investigation, Ettore needed someone unusual to deliver the goods, so he picked a woman no one would suspect as having anything to do with him."

"The other women didn't want anything to do with him either," Lucia muttered.

Gio knew that, but there was a difference between them and Lucia. "You have family, a community who cares, who would miss you. You said yourself that they didn't."

Lucia's jaw tightened. "He knew I had someone he could use to coerce me."

"And a stellar reputation. He sends you to Gennaro with the ring and no one would be the wiser. Including you. Because, as you recall, you didn't even know you had it."

Lucia pulled the chain at her neck, revealing the St. Christopher. Gio's heart skipped a beat. She was drawing comfort from the gift. She raised her eyes to his. "What would Gennaro have done to me if I'd just delivered the ring?"

Gio swallowed. He didn't want to tell her what he really thought. "He might have let you go. Gennaro has a reputation for being generous." Until he wasn't.

Miles shifted in his chair. Ugo grumbled to himself. Gio let the silence hang in the air, giving Lucia time to digest all he'd told her.

Finally, she asked, "Why can't we just give him the ring?"

"It's not his, Lucia. Touhy's goons stole it from the Charlotte mail truck, but whose it was originally, I don't know. I'm not sure they had it legally, either, since there's no agency searching for it."

"Then how are we going to end this?"

"If we meet Ettore on his turf in Chicago, then he'll just buy his freedom and come after us with even more vengeance, so we're going to settle this here. In Eagle."

Lucia raised an eyebrow. "Is the Eagle police force up for this level of criminal?"

Gio had the same thought, considering the way Lily's situation had played out in October. This time, however, not only was Joey on their side, but he would know all the details. "Joey is going to coordinate with the local chief of police. Miles will run security. You and your grandfather will be safe. Once we have Ettore in custody, he won't bother us again." Meaning Gennaro would take care of him.

"What about Gennaro?" Had Lucia read his mind? "Won't he still want the ring?"

"He might, but with the heat on it, he will have to get it a different way. And when he learns the authorities have it, there's no reason to come after you." He hoped. "Right now you are a pawn in an evil man's game. We're changing the rules and bringing the situation to a close."

"I don't see this going well." Lucia shook her head.

"We don't have much choice. This needs to end, and better it ends here where the police aren't corrupt than in Chicago where Ettore will go free."

"He could still buy off the police here."

"No. Joey was one of those officers. It's too small a department for that to happen. You remember Miles worked as a sniper? I trust him with my life, and more importantly, I trust him with yours."

Lucia pressed her lips together—he must stop noticing them—her fingers drummed the table. "What are you going to do?"

"Stay right by your side because, while I do trust Miles, I won't let you go through this alone."

Before Lucia could reply, the crunch of tires outside had Miles and Gio on their feet.

"It's Joey." Miles jogged outside.

Gio requested Lucia and Ugo stay inside while he followed his friend. The sun cast long shadows and a bank of clouds sat heavy on the western horizon. Gio turned up the collar of his coat as against the wind, wishing he remembered his scarf.

Katy met them at Joey's car.

"What's wrong?" Miles demanded of Joey.

"Someone threw a brick through the creamery's window." Joey planted his hands on his hips. "My brother-in-law is hounding the police to find the culprit before the truce falls apart."

"First Lily's dogs. Now Andy's plant?" Miles rubbed his chin, producing the familiar rasping sound of a no-shave day. "Is someone trying to stir up the community again?"

"It's putting me on edge." Joey rammed his hands in his pockets, glanced at Gio. "And we're baiting a Chicago thug into the middle of it."

"I won't be the reason for bringing danger into the town." Lucia joined the group. Gio hadn't even heard her leave the house. "There are innocent people here. They do not deserve to become victims."

"Yes, there are innocent people with regards to your situation, but they are not angels," Joey said. "Violence could break out again, and it would have nothing to do with your Chicago connection. But his presence here when the town could combust again ... I'm afraid our protection measures might not be enough."

"Are you sure Ettore will come himself?" Miles asked Gio,

Gio nodded. "He was willing to question Ugo, Lucia's grandfather, himself. He can't risk one of his goons keeping the ring. He'll be the one." But he'd undoubtedly bring muscle.

"Right." Katy rubbed her arms. "It be too cold to stand out here. Inside with all of ya."

Joey took her hand, and Miles didn't hesitate to follow them inside, but Lucia didn't move and so Gio stayed with her. Lucia tugged on her coat, a threadbare one that had seen too many winters. Gio slid his arm over her shoulder and pulled her close. She didn't balk; in fact, she seemed to tuck in closer.

"*Buon compleanno*, Lucia. Happy birthday." He lowered his chin so he could see her, but as he spoke, she raised her face to his, bringing her lips within a hair's breadth of his.

Her eyes widened, but she didn't move. A white puff of breath wisped between them. Cold stiffened his extremities, and he flexed his fingers. So many reasons to put space between them, but he had no desire to entertain them. He ran his gaze over Lucia's olive skin, dipped to her lips, then up to her warm, brown eyes. They searched his own, neither pushing forward nor retreating, letting him decide whether he was done denying the truth to himself.

Si, this woman, she was special to him. He slid his hand down Lucia's back, drawing her nearer until her lips touched his. Si, si. More special than any other. And one light kiss was not enough. He wouldn't hurt her, though, no matter his feelings, and made to pull away. Only, she lifted on her toes to reach for him.

He wrapped both arms around her, tight as could be, and deepened their kiss. Si, si, he cared for this woman so deeply, he could feel it in his soul. The kiss merely brought the emotions he'd attempted to bury to the surface. Emotions he'd left to simmer so that this spark ignited them in a powerful explosion.

He rocked back on his heels. Leveled. What would become of their relationship now that he'd blown up their friendship with a heart-rending kiss?

Chapter 10

Lucia smiled at her grandfather. He sat at Katy's kitchen table, illuminated by the kerosene lamp at its center, a cup of coffee halfway to his mouth. *"Com'è il caffè?"*

"Squisito." Nonno raised one hand, fingers pressed to his thumb. *"Complimenti."*

Lucia put away the last dish, having assured Katy she would clean up supper when Katy's veterinary services called her out to a local farm. Contentment rested like a shawl over Lucia's shoulders. She tried to convince herself that it was simply the ability to spend the rest of her birthday with Nonno, but if she allowed herself to be honest, it had everything to do with Gio's kiss.

"What are you thinking?" Nonno's gravelly Italian pulled Lucia from her reverie.

"I am glad you are here." Lucia wiped down the table, Nonno lifting his cup so she could wash beneath it.

"Hmm. I think it is someone else." Nonno captured the hand that held the wet cloth. "I saw you two. Through the window."

Heat rose in Lucia's cheeks.

"It makes me happy. Gio Vella is a good man. A good man for you. You like him, yes?"

There was no use denying it. She missed him and he'd only been gone for two hours. Gio had left with Miles and Joey to make their arrangements for the evening. Joey planned to watch the dairy plant, Miles planned to watch Lily's barn, and Gio planned to watch Katy's house. Lucia and Katy had tried to tell them they couldn't manage on so little sleep and spread so thin, but heroes that they were, they couldn't sit idly by when there was something they could do to help. If only Lucia knew what she could do, too.

"Why do you not tell him how you feel?" Nonno's question derailed her train of thought.

"I couldn't do that. It is not my place. And he doesn't feel that way about me. It would only cause embarrassment." Except that he'd kissed her.

"That boy is so caught up in taking care of everyone else he can't see that he needs someone to take care of him." Nonno folded his arms. "And you're too nice to him about it."

"What?" Lucia took a step back.

"I'm saying you two need to talk. Relationships only survive because of communication."

Lucia dunked the cloth into the dishwater, then wrung it out and hung it up to dry. She'd tried to broach the topic when Gio first brought her to Eagle. Could she do it again? It would have to be an impulsive move because if she tried to plan it, she'd chicken out.

"I'm going to bed now." Nonno rose. "The travel has made me sleepy."

"Of course, Nonno."

"Gio will be here tonight. You will talk to him?"

Lucia took his coffee cup without a word.

"Lucia? Promise me."

"Why does this matter so much to you, Nonno?"

He circled the table and put his callused hands on her cheeks. "Because I want to know you have someone to look after you when I cannot."

Tears pricked Lucia's eyes. "Surely, you will be here for many, many more years." But he had been ailing more lately.

"I'm getting old, Nipotina."

"But—"

"No. Do not fret for me. Only promise to talk to Gio."

Lucia nodded, but her heart pounded.

Nonno kissed her cheeks, wished her a happy birthday, and then left her alone in the dim room.

Unsettled, Lucia made swift work of washing Nonno's cup. With nothing else to wash, she donned her coat and lifted the wash bucket, lumbering under its weight to the door. Discarding the old water, she refilled it with fresh water from Katy's pump. The night air was crisp and cold. It stung her nose and tingled her fingers. No stars peeked through the clouds above. In fact, if she wasn't mistaken, the night smelled of snow.

She rubbed the St. Christopher that hung from her neck and pictured the life she and Gio could have together. She had no doubt his family would welcome her—they'd already welcomed Nonno. Between Gio's connections and his brothers, Lucia would definitely be safe. And she had no doubt Gio would provide for her. All these reasons made him a great choice for a husband. Not to mention how handsome he was.

They were also the same reasons every other unmarried young woman in their neighborhood set their sights on him. So, as much as Lucia had feelings for Gio—feelings she hadn't allowed herself to name—she wouldn't entertain more with him if he didn't feel the same way about her. If he didn't choose her.

When Gio returned, could she really fulfill her promise to Nonno and talk openly and honestly with Gio? Could she tell him how she felt? And if he didn't think of her the same way she thought of him, it would be the end of a dream. Then what should she do?

She lifted the wash bucket to return inside. No need to think these thoughts in the cold. She was nearly to the back steps when a car turned into the yard. Gio must be back already. Or was it another farmer looking for Katy? It could also be Emberto, though would he know where she was so soon?

Her heart picked up speed. She wouldn't wait outside to find out.

Gio shouldered his knapsack and hurried into Mrs. St. Thomas's kitchen only to find Miles scrubbing the floor. "Mio amico?"

Miles looked up with a sheepish expression. "I startled Mrs. St. Thomas again, and she dropped the eggs she planned to use to make more cookies. You leaving?"

"Si, si."

Miles stood. Rinsed the cloth he'd used. "I want to help more than I am. You cannot defend against Ettore alone."

"Giglia needs you. I understand."

"Andy plans to relieve Joey at midnight. I'll have him stay with Lily so I can check in."

"That is not necessary."

"You know it is. Two are better than one, especially if Ettore brings muscle."

Gio's shoulders sagged.

"Plenty more!" Mrs. St. Thomas bustled into the room carrying a basket. "No need to ask another farm for them."

Miles reddened. "I'm terribly sorry."

"And I have a way you can repay me." Mrs. St. Thomas set the basket on the table and put her hands on her hips. "You can be Joseph in my nativity. I've decided it's the best option."

"*Your* nativity?" Miles winked at her.

She blustered and Miles laughed. Gio considered slipping out the door, but a look from Miles stopped him.

"I have a much better idea, ma'am." The gleam in Miles's eyes had Gio wishing he'd run when he had the chance. "I heard Lucia will be your Mary."

"She is?" The words were out before Gio could stop them. Lucia didn't strike him as someone who would enjoy participating in that type of Christmas tradition. She seemed like she would much prefer to stay behind the scenes.

"Katy insisted she would be perfect." Mrs. St. Thomas shrugged. "And paired with Miles, I have no qualms about asking a foreigner."

Gio bristled at the older woman's generalization. Lucia was no more foreign than the president.

"I think you should pair her with Gio." Miles didn't cover his smirk before Gio caught sight of it.

"No, no." Gio stepped back, bumping into the doorframe. "I do not—"

"You would match Lucia." Mrs. St. Thomas eyed him, then turned her scrutiny on Miles. "You trust this one?"

"With my life, ma'am."

Gio opened his mouth to protest.

"Good." Mrs. St. Thomas snatched her egg basket. "Then out of my kitchen, both of you. I have cookies to bake."

Miles grinned.

"And you." Mrs. St. Thomas speared Gio with her finger. "Be at the church at four on Christmas Eve or Miles will pay the price."

"I don't want to know what that means," Miles whispered to Gio as they escaped the kitchen. "So don't be late."

"I can't—"

"Because it's Lucia?" Miles folded his massive arms, making him look even bigger. He'd never intimidated Gio before, but with his tone and stance directed at Gio the way it was, a strange quiver shimmied up Gio's back.

He squared his shoulders. "I do not need a matchmaker."

"You do, my friend, because you can't get out of your own way."

Fortunately, the hall phone rang in time to save him from attempting to respond. Miles answered it and Gio headed for the door.

"It's for you." Miles stopped him. "Your brother."

Gio leapt for the phone. "What news do you have?" he asked in Italian, hoping the operator wouldn't understand.

"I found the owner. He didn't know the package was missing at first because he sent it to his daughter as a surprise anniversary gift."

"Fine. I'll speak with him when I return." Check one adversary off the list. "Is that everything?"

"In a hurry?" His brother's tease easily carried over the phone line.

"Yes. He could be here at any time."

"That's actually true. He slipped the officers we had on him sometime this afternoon."

Gio's heart rate picked up speed. "And you didn't lead with that?"

"You wouldn't have heard me about the package."

Gio muttered to himself about older brothers. "Is that all?"

"Be safe. Ettore didn't leave alone. At least four of his men are unaccounted for."

Ending the call, Gio whispered a prayer before telling Miles the news. Miles promised to get Lily and Joey so Joey could escort Lily and Katy to a safe place while Miles helped Gio keep watch. The local police would have to manage the cheese plant alone.

Gio drove to Katy's home. His breath fogged the windshield as he prayed for Lucia's protection, for God to slow Ettore so Gio would reach Lucia first. The idea of losing Lucia struck him like a cudgel to the stomach. He'd always thought fondly of her, but the past few days he experienced feelings for her that he had never allowed himself to feel before. And that kiss. She was a woman to be cherished.

But, he told Ugo from the very beginning, he was not the man for someone as sweet as Lucia. He operated in the shadows, she in the light. She stayed to care for her family. Gio left. He might be able to find things, people, even romance—all for others—but he never deserved any of it himself. It would never repay the damage he did that day in Central Park.

No cars were in Katy's yard, including her truck. Not a sliver of moonlight shone through the clouds. It made it difficult to see, but also to be seen. Gio liked it that way. His time as a scout taught him how to use this environment, but at the sight of the open back door, Gio barely set the brake before he was racing toward the house. He managed to stop himself before he ascended the steps. Best not to rush inside and lose the one advantage he had—surprise.

A form appeared in the doorway before he could retreat. "Gio?" A broom dropped between them.

Lucia! "You are safe?" He ran his gaze over her, looking for any hint of injury, taking in her winter coat, mittens. "You are not under coerc—" Why could he never think of the word?

"Duress?" She lifted a lantern between them and he didn't miss that her hand shook. Panic carved new lines in her beautiful face. The muscles of her neck constricted. "I—"

He touched her shoulder. "What's wrong? Is Emberto here?"

Lucia shook her head, but her trembling didn't dissipate. "Yours was the car I heard."

"Katy?" he asked.

"Out on a call." She looked everywhere but at him, a snowflake landed on her cheek, and a sinking feeling washed over him.

"What is it? I am here. I will protect you." He touched her cheek to find it cold. "I will not let Emberto hurt you."

She backed away. "Maybe we should go inside."

Yes. But he couldn't let this go. Something wasn't right. And, having eliminated the possibility of danger, he guessed it was something between them. Was it the kiss? Gio rubbed his chest. This was all his fault. He'd caused her to be uncomfortable with him.

"Nonno is asleep. I'll make coffee for you."

"Wait." He snatched her free hand and pulled her close. Thankfully, she didn't resist. "The kiss ... mi dispiace."

"I don't want an apology." Lucia yanked away and gathered up the broom she'd dropped at their feet before facing him again. "I want ... I want ..."

He studied her as snowflakes fell between, trying to anticipate what she needed from him. She leaned the broom just inside the door and set the lantern on the ground, casting her eyes in shadow. Her breath puffed a small cloud and she shifted her feet, but did not move their conversation inside.

When it seemed she wouldn't finish her sentence without prompting, he forced himself to ask. "What do you want, Lucia? You can tell me."

She pulled out the St. Christopher, her chin on her chest. Snow left a crown of white on her dark curls. "I love you, Gio."

Gio choked on his swallow. Lucia loved him?

She raised her chin. "I have for a long time, I think. I don't expect you to feel that way about me, but I want you to know. The kiss. It meant something to me."

Did it mean something to you? He could read the question as it danced through her eyes.

Gio's jaw loosened, his thoughts careening through his head. For all his flirting, all his matchmaking, he had no idea what to say. How did he tell her the kiss meant something to him too? That he wished he was a good enough man so he could act on how he felt toward her. That she deserved to love someone better. Someone ... else. Yet he didn't want to let her go.

Lucia gave him a sad smile that pierced his heart. "I'll be inside making coffee."

He shook his head. What was he doing, letting her walk away? "Lucia, wait."

She spun on her toes, expectancy lighting her eyes. Mamma mia, she did love him. And wanted him to love her back.

"Well, isn't this a cozy scene." Ettore's voice came from behind him as cold metal pressed into Gio's neck.

Lucia gasped and Gio's heart thudded. He'd done it again. He'd allowed his emotions to distract him, and now he'd put another woman at risk. The gun pushed against his skull, forcing him to his knees. He dropped his mittens, hiding them under his leg and digging them into the snow, then raised his hands.

The fear in Lucia's eyes fired his determination. Si, si, he loved this woman. Loved her enough to put himself between her and Ettore. He'd suffer anything to stall for as long as Ettore let him live in hopes Miles could get to Lucia before Ettore doused the innocent light in her eyes.

Chapter 11

Lucia shivered, her back scraping against the trunk of a tree to which she was tied. While she'd been allowed to sit, Gio currently stood facing a tree not ten feet away, his arms stretched around it and his wrists secured with rope. A lantern illuminated the darkness between them. Beyond the glow, woods surrounded them.

If she hadn't missed her guess, they'd been taken but a few miles from Katy's house. On foot. However, snow had been falling since Emberto surprised them on Katy's back step and dragged them to this remote area, the fresh precipitation covering their tracks. Usually, the snow would feel romantic as if softly drifted through the trees overhead ...

She wrapped her arms around her knees and tried to stop her teeth from chattering and her tears from falling. Thankfully, she hadn't removed her coat before opening the door to Gio, but she had no hat or mittens, and the cold had long since numbed her extremities. Gio also had his coat, unbuttoned as it was to allow Emberto to land the fourteen punches—yes, she counted each one—to Gio's stomach.

Wind whipped the snow into a swirl, partially covering the blood which had dripped from Gio's nose and mouth. Emberto's shadow caused her to raise her head. His knuckles were torn from where they'd hit Gio's face exactly eight times.

"You'll tell me where the ring is, won't you?" He sneered. "To protect your amore."

"Do not touch her." Gio spat into the snow. "I did not tell her where it is. Only I know."

Emberto spun on him, spraying snow in Lucia's face. "Are you willing to go to your grave with that secret? You won't be here to protect her once you're dead."

Lucia saw the hesitation in Gio's eyes, but it was only a flash, and then it was replaced with the same icy glare he'd maintained since Emberto first pressed a gun to his head. Why hadn't she seen Emberto approach? Why had she let her emotions distract her from her surroundings when she knew Emberto could be around the corner? This was all her fault.

"Convince him, would you?" Emberto rolled his eyes back toward Lucia. "Because when I come back, I'm going to kill him." Emberto waved to his goons and they disappeared into the trees, leaving the lantern behind.

Lucia tugged at the rope holding her pinned against the tree.

"Do not struggle." Gio's words stopped her movement. "The knots, they will only tighten."

"Then what can I do? How do we escape?" Between dying of the cold or at Emberto's hand, she didn't know which was worse. "I can't see you suffer any more."

"That is what he wants, Lucia. Be strong." He coughed and groaned.

"No." Lucia fought the rope. It scraped against her coat, which gave her an idea. It was risky, but it might just work.

"Lucia, they will be back." The panic in Gio's voice as he lapsed into Italian drove her. "They are likely listening even now. Please save your strength."

Lucia ignored him as she unbuttoned her coat and worked to open it, freeing the fabric from between the rope and her chest.

"Lucia, please. I cannot do this again."

She froze. "Do what again?"

Gio rested his bruised face against the tree, the lantern light casting him in a ghoulish shadow. "I was in love with a girl back in New York, but the tenements, the pressure to be like my brothers ... and America had just entered the war."

Lucia held perfectly still, unsure what to do with his story.

"She wanted to get married, wanted to marry a policeman." Gio forged on despite the pain etching his face. "I told her I would never be a policeman like my brothers, but I would be a soldier. Standing there in Central Park, I begged her to wait for me, to see how brave I would be." His voice broke.

She tossed her coat aside, and the extra give in the rope provided just enough wiggle room to twist the knot around to where she could reach it. She had to get free if for no other reason than to wrap her arms around this man who meant so much to her.

"Mamma moved the family to Chicago during the flu epidemic, so when my brothers returned from the war, they never went back to New York." Gio grimaced. "But I did and I was too late. She had indeed married a policeman. And then didn't survive the Red Summer of '19."

"Oh, Gio." She had to get this knot untied. She had to comfort him. "That's when you came to Chicago." It all made sense to her now—his resistance to the matchmaking attempts and his desire to help everyone he met.

"I did not need to go to war, Lucia. Two years. Two years and the war would have been over by the time I turned eighteen. I could have married her. Protected her. She would have gone to Chicago with my family and not been in New York to be killed. But my need to get away from the tenements, to better myself, to be different than my brothers ..." He sucked in a breath. "I put myself before her, and it got her killed."

"Gio." Her heart broke for him.

"I won't do it again. Your safety comes before anything else."

Tears slipped down her cheeks. "Including your feelings for me? Because you do have feelings for me, don't you?"

He groaned. "I can't, Lucia, don't you see that?" He coughed, his moan bringing more tears to her eyes.

"You stay with me, Gio."

She met his eyes, willing her strength into him. Then she went to work on the knot. Snow fell around them, heavy and insistent. The forest was silent, peaceful, as if welcoming them to lie down and sleep in peace. No. That was not the peace they needed. They needed heavenly peace to calm them enough to think clearly. Yes. Heavenly peace.

When Gio's head lulled to the side, she began to sing. Quietly at first, then stronger, letting the words of "Silent Night" weave between them. Gio had been strong for her, to protect her. In return, she would protect his spirit, his soul for as long as they had. No despair. No giving up. They would fight until the end.

Finally, the rope fell away from her raw fingers. They throbbed, but in a numb way, making her thankful for the cold. She stumbled to her feet, her legs refusing to cooperate. But she forced them to obey. Gio hadn't spoken since she began to sing, and now she feared she hadn't made the right choice. Maybe she'd put him to sleep, which could be deadly in these conditions.

"Oh, Gio."

His eyes fluttered open. In the barest of whispers, he said something about lying. Or dying?

"Say it again." She pressed closer, desperate to hear him.

"Blade. Coat lining." *Lining*!

Lucia ran her hands along the open sides where the buttons and holes were, hurrying before Emberto returned. "Where? I can't find it."

"Back hem." His coat hung almost to his knees. She circled behind him and ran her fingers along the bottom stitching. There! The tiniest of bulges. Using her teeth since her fingers had stopped working, she tore the threads away, letting a small blade drop into her hand.

"Hold on, Gio." She attacked the rope that held him.

"They will return."

"Then we must be faster." The rope frayed beneath each pass of the blade.

"Leave me. Run."

"Not without you."

"How sweet." Emberto's chuckle shot fear through her. Not just fear. Something else. Something a lot stronger. She slipped the blade into Gio's hand.

"*Non*, Lucia." Gio tugged at his bindings.

Lucia put herself squarely between him and Emberto. She would neither let Emberto touch Gio, nor see the half-cut rope. "Do not touch him again."

With one step, Emberto towered over her, and with one swipe, he sent her tumbling into the snow beside the lantern.

"Lucia!" Gio's shout ended with a cough and a moan.

Emberto hauled her to her feet, pulling her close and shoving his face into hers. "Tell him to tell me where he hid the ring."

"No." Lucia glared back, sensing Emberto's men circling them. If she could keep their focus on her for a few minutes more, Gio would be free.

"I must have that ring!" He shook her with each word, and Lucia clenched her teeth to keep from biting her tongue.

A gun cocked. "Release her."

Gio?

Emberto put her in front of him like a shield, a gun to her head. "You willing to lose her, Vella?"

Gio leaned against the tree, shredded ropes lying at its trunk beside one of Emberto's unconscious guards, a gun steady in his hand. "You kill her, you die."

"No. You will die." Emberto pressed the gun harder against her skin, but Lucia refused to make a noise. If the toe of her boot could reach it, dare she snuff out the lantern?

"That outcome, it is inevitable."

Lucia frowned. No, it wasn't. Gio wasn't going to die. Not if she had anything to say about it. She sent an elbow into Emberto's gut and dropped to the snow. Gunfire rang through the air, and Lucia curled into a tighter ball, covering her head, her ears. Whimpers slipped out despite her best efforts.

Please, God, don't let Gio die. Please.

Gio didn't get one shot off before bullets tore into the tree he'd whirled himself behind. He had to get to Lucia. Or draw the men away. He nearly snapped his fingers. That was it!

Crouching low, he dodged to the next tree, staying in the shadows even as he tried to reach the lantern light. Shouts rang out behind him. More gunfire. He pressed his back against a tree as bark sprayed past him. His ribs ached so that each breath burned like fire. His face pulsed. He'd prefer not to add a gunshot wound to the mix, but if that's what it took to save Lucia ...

He prepared to dart to another tree.

"Police!" The shout buckled Gio's knees. "Hands! Hands! Hands!"

Gunfire cracked around him, but it was the slicing sound of a rifle shot that brought up his head. Miles had found his clues. His mittens. His hat. His scarf. Within moments, he heard Emberto's surrender, accompanied by a painful moan. Gio released a slow breath. He would have defied his stand on guns to save Lucia, but thank God, he hadn't had to fire.

"Gio." Miles suddenly knelt before him, his rifle slung behind his back, and raised a blindingly bright flashlight. "You look ..."

"Bad." Gio couldn't grin—it hurt too much. "Lucia?"

"Lily is with her." Miles lowered the light.

"Giglia?" There could be no way Miles would purposefully bring her to a gunfight.

"She's a better shot than me and you know it."

Gio couldn't hide his surprise no matter how painful it was to move his facial muscles.

"Chief deputized the twins and me. Pieter tracked you." Miles squeezed Gio's shoulder. "We'll get you to a doctor."

"Lucia." Gio tried to stand, but his legs wouldn't hold him.

"Stay. I'll get her."

And then she was there. Eyes red from crying, nose red from the cold, cheeks pale as the snow still swirling around them. But she was here and she was beautiful. Tears ran over his tender face, and he realized he could only see her with one eye. But she was alive and whole and safe.

She reached out to touch his bruised cheek. "Gio."

He hauled her into his arms and carefully buried his face in her neck. "*Sei tutto per me.*" *You are everything to me.* She held him as tightly as he held her until throats clearing lightened her hold, but she stayed close, supporting him, and Gio didn't want to let her go.

"He did a job on you." The chief—Gio remembered the man from when Miles had been shot—shook his head. "You boys always manage to save the girl, but I'd thank you to stop trying to die in the process."

"That's a good plan, Chief." Joey strode up. "Ettore and his goons are headed back to lock up."

"I'll un-deputize Wright and Lily, but I'm of a mind to ignore your resignation, Moore. I want you back."

Lily elbowed her brother and Miles gave an encouraging smile.

"I'll think on it, sir." Joey held out a hand to his former boss. "First, let's get Gio to the doc."

"What of the ring?" Miles asked as he wrapped one of Gio's arms around his neck, forcing Lucia to move aside, while Joey took his other arm. Miles used his flashlight to light their way.

"I will return it to the owner." Gio spoke through clenched teeth, the movement tortuous.

"Do you know who the owner is?" Lucia followed behind.

"Gio learned just before he left for Katy's," Miles said. "You both can return it when—"

"No." Gio interrupted his friend's planning. "It is not yet safe."

"Why?" Joey asked. "Ettore isn't getting off this time.

Lucia was silent and it worried Gio, but he spoke his piece, his muddled head making the English nearly impossible. "Ettore, he was hired. I must first assure it is safe."

Lucia huffed. "No one will bother me now. There is no reason once everyone knows I do not have the ring."

"We do not know for certain." If only he could face her, explain without Miles and Joey propping him up, without his head pounding and the effort of speaking being excruciating. "I will go."

"You will go." Lucia's voice wavered. "In the state you are? When will you ask for help, Gio? When will you let someone find something for *you?*"

What? He was trying to help *her*.

"Miles and Joey, you take him to the doctor. Lily will see me home." She sounded strangled.

Gio had to see her expression. "Lucia, wait." He tried to free himself, but Miles and Joey would not relinquish their hold on him.

She didn't help matters by staying behind him. "We can talk when you are no longer in pain."

"Lucia."

"Horsefeathers, Vella," Joey muttered. "I know I say stupid things, but even I can see what you just said was utter foolishness."

"He's right." The censure in Miles's voice put Gio on his guard. "You're my brother, and I care about you too much not to speak up when you hurt someone. Can't you see Lucia wants to help you? Be your partner in ending this threat?"

Gio bowed his head, shame and conviction warring with the fear in his heart. "It's her safety I cannot risk. Not again."

"You love her." Miles adjusted Gio's arm over his shoulder. When Gio didn't respond, Miles sighed. "You tell her yet?"

No. He had no doubt as to her feelings, but was he ready to let go of the past so they could have a future?

Chapter 12

Sunday, December 24

Ten days. Gio adjusted the collar of his coat as he dodged the wind whistling down the alley beside the warehouse where Signore Gennaro kept his offices. It had taken Gio ten days to find who first hired Charles Connors to steal the ring, then Emberto Ettore to kill Connors and transport the ring the rest of the way.

Gio had left Eagle the day after Emberto's arrest. Miles's rebuke rang in his ears. Lucia's stoic pain echoed in his heart. No, Ettore didn't dim the light in her eyes. Gio managed to do that all on his own. It was why he left. He couldn't sit still. With the incessant pain in his chest, whether physical or emotional or a combination, he couldn't manage having Lucia and her kindness nurse him back to health.

Especially after he hurt her.

And so he left to be a hero. Just like New York.

His shoes echoed in the empty warehouse. All the barrels filled with illegal alcohol were gone, and nothing yet had taken its place. A good thing, in Gio's mind. He was tired of having the sins of others on his conscience. He'd already unloaded all of what he knew to his brother only to discover that he didn't witness anything specific enough to lead to the arrest of any of the criminals in the city. Then why did it still bother him?

He closed a fist around the ring in his pocket. The owner, a Mr. Cooper-Hill, had been relieved to have it discovered, but had no desire to fulfill his original plan for it, considering the criminals who had handled it. He must have been exceedingly wealthy to claim his daughter would be better off with a different piece of jewelry and to instead give it to Gio as a finder's reward. The man might have money to waste on such superstitions, but Gio had no such ideas. He would use the gift. If he survived this meeting.

Two goons stood on either side of Gennaro's door. They patted Gio down and then one allowed him to enter. The gaunt man sat behind his desk, a gun resting beside a pile of papers. Gio took a slow breath, willing the pain in his ribs to allow him to think.

Mamma had insisted on taking care of him over the last ten days, and his brothers had limited his activities as only older brothers could. And so he'd had ten days to figure out how to eliminate the risk to Lucia for good. It came down to this meeting, which would either end the threat or end him.

"Signore Vella." Gennaro's hand inched toward the pistol. "Do you have my ring?"

"I have a proposition." The man's eyebrows rose, as Gio wanted them to, then Gio switched to Italian to drive home his plan. "I come with a bargain for innocent lives."

"Speak plainly."

"Women, our women, are being used, sold, and otherwise mistreated because they have no one to look out for them. Homeless, jobless, with no one to miss them, they are taken from the streets—our streets—and I want them left alone."

"Tall order. We need to fill our businesses."

"The women who do not want to be a part of those businesses need to be given another option."

"And you have such an option."

"Will you give me one?"

Gennaro squinted.

"I'm looking to purchase one of the abandoned buildings to create a home for these women. They'd work there for their room and board. Eventually, this depression will be over and they will be able to get jobs. They can stay as long as they need without the fear of being lured off the street. They'd be under my protection. And the protection of my brothers."

"What do I get out of it?"

"The honor of doing something right. Because that's the other thing that's changing. From here on out, if I see a crime, I'm testifying."

He laid a hand on the gun. "You have a death wish?"

"Keeping the innocent alive and fed isn't enough anymore. A woman ..." Gio faltered. "The woman I love was targeted in all of this. An innocent woman. It was not enough to make sure she had food to feed her grandfather. She needed protection, safety. She's not alone in that need."

Gennaro tapped his fingers on the desk. "You love her, do you?"

"She doesn't know yet." He nodded to the gun. "You going to let me tell her?"

"Love makes a man do foolish things."

The way Gennaro said those words made Gio fall silent. Shallow breaths kept the pain in his ribs at bay. At least enough for him to think. Love had him walking into a lion's den, and he did love Lucia. He could finally admit that to himself, but would it be enough to overcome his fear? Would his actions today be enough?

"Yes, love makes a man do foolish things. Like steal a ring from his wife's ex-lover." Gennaro lifted the phone on his desk and spoke into the receiver. "Come down here."

Gio shifted away from the door, balancing on the balls of his feet. He might as well be a cornered rabbit—an injured one, no less. Another minute of tense silence and heels clacked their way toward the door. Gio braced for the visitor. The door opened inward, blocking his view at first. Then came the *swoosh* of fabric, the dark blue of a skirt worn by a woman of middle age.

"Yes, darling?" She smiled at Gennaro.

Gennaro stood and a look crossed his eyes that Gio could only classify as adoration, but it was so quick, he couldn't be sure. However, it did explain much.

"I'd like to introduce you to Gio Vella." Gennaro turned to him, welcoming him into the conversation. "Signore Vella, meet my wife."

"Signora." Gio bowed.

"You are the infamous Gio Vella?" She stalked closer until her skirts met his legs. "They say you are a flirt."

Gio took a step back.

"He's in love, darling," Gennaro said from his desk.

"A pity." Signora Gennaro sighed but gave Gio a few feet of space. "Why must I meet him?"

"He has a proposition that you will want to hear."

She returned her attention to Gio and he told her what he'd told her husband about creating a refuge for women who wished to avoid a life of prostitution.

"I'd hate to lose my girls." Signora Gennaro tapped a finger to red lips.

Gio absorbed her words. She was the madam in Gennaro's operation! "Were you going to force Lucia into that life?" The question burst out louder than his ribs liked, nearly forcing out a moan.

She glanced back at her husband. "He *is* in love."

Gio started to protest. "That has nothing—"

"Come, come." She cupped his chin, but Gio didn't dare move. "You've been content to let the Mafioso do their crime as long as they let you feed the innocent and heal the wounded. Deciding to interfere directly with business, that is foolish, and it can only mean two things—you found religion, which I already know you have, or you found love."

Gio's heart pounded.

"You realize what it means to go against us."

Gio nodded as much as he could with her fingers still holding his chin and slid his hand into his pocket to grip his diamond ticket out of here. He'd use it here if he must—though he hated to hand it over to thieves willing to kill for it—but he really needed it to finance Lucia's plans, if these two agreed.

"We're not truly going against one another." Gio forced his shoulders to relax. "I'm still aiming to protect the vulnerable, the innocent. I always have, and I know it's why you have let me live—because at the end of the day, you might have a business to run, but for some reason, you also care about your fellow immigrants." Like Capone, in prison for his crimes and yet funding bread lines. "I'd appreciate it if you would pass the word along that my desire to help those in need has not changed, only widened. Or perhaps deepened."

"This was her idea, wasn't it?"

"Her desire, my plan and execution." Gio swallowed on that last word, his eyes darting to the gun once more—and then the realization hit him like a bullet. He was scared to love Lucia and yet he was willing to face torture and death for her and her dreams. It was time to give God his fear so he could finally experience for himself the joy he spread to others. If Lucia would have him.

He tightened his grip on the ring in his pocket. He had a deal to survive so he could make it to the live nativity in time to be Lucia's Joseph and tell her the truth about how he felt towards her.

Lucia ran a hand down Glenn's nose as they stood on the outskirts of the town center, a few blocks from the church. The entire section of the main street had been closed for the live nativity processional that would occur at precisely nine in the evening—leaving her ten minutes to convince Mrs. St. Thomas and Miles that Lily should take her place as Mary.

"How's Glenn?" The big man beside her offered a tower of protection, but she missed Gio. When he first left, Katy consoled her and doctored her aching soul, however, it had been Lily who gave her hope that all was not lost between him and Lucia. The woman spoke of being afraid to love and yet she loved Miles wholeheartedly because *perfect love casts out fear*.

"I think he'd be more comfortable with Lily." She refused to look at Miles, knowing her cheeks would darken after thinking about his relationship with Lily.

"Lily is enjoying your grandfather's company. She misses hers."

Lucia ignored the pang that thought caused. "Are you trying to guilt me into playing Mary?" This time she gave him a side-eye.

Miles chuckled. "He'll be here."

"And if he's not?" Lucia had been debating returning to Chicago without waiting for Gio's return, but transportation was a problem, and Nonno had seemed freshly rejuvenated under Katy's care. And Lily's. Miles was right, the two women must have had a good relationship with their grandfathers to miss them so much that they would adopt Nonno as their own. It had delayed Lucia's determination to return to Chicago. Because, honestly, what did she have waiting for her there? Her whole life was with Nonno.

"Two cows, four sheep, three goats, and one little donkey." Katy appeared with a paper and pencil, her humongous black beast of a horse following her like a puppy. "I declined the pig. Ten animals is enough for this stable."

"No chickens?" Miles grinned. "Or dogs?"

Katy shook her head. "After the episode with Lily's dogs at the Christmas pageant, no more chaos."

"Did you find out who let them loose?" Lucia scratched Glenn between the ears.

"No." Miles frowned. "No one has bothered them or the dairy plant."

She heard what he didn't say, that it had been too quiet. Sometimes silence was a bad thing. "Hopefully, tonight will go smoothly. Another reason why Lily should ride Glenn. Or Katy, you could."

"No, no." Katy laughed. "I love me Glenn, but you are Mary tonight."

Lucia rubbed the St. Christopher hanging from her neck.

"He'll be here." Miles nudged her arm.

Katy folded her arms. "Do ya want him to be here?"

The question took Lucia aback. "Of course I ..." Her defensiveness caused her words to fade. All week, she'd been so focused on whether Gio loved her enough to return that she hadn't considered whether she should let him back into her life. Was it wise? After he declined her help, after he left without a word? She sighed.

"Och, ya love the man." Katy pulled her into a hug. "But don't let that be clouding your judgment."

Lucia made eye contact with Miles, who still wore a frown, and asked the question that had dogged her since Gio left. "Have my ... feelings ... for him been entirely one sided? I know he cares, but ..." *Does he love me as I love him?*

"He does." Miles rubbed his scruff. "But I wish I knew whether that was enough."

Lucia absorbed his words. If Gio's love wasn't the question, then did he think he had to earn her love?

"It's time!" Mrs. St. Thomas clapped her hands. "Everyone ready?"

She'd organized the nativity to begin with a procession down Main Street, which was lined with candle-holding neighbors. First cows and goats, led by farmers, then the sheep along with children singing the Christmas hymns they'd sang during the Christmas pageant, and lastly, Mary, Joseph, and Glenn. They would end at the makeshift stable the men had built in the churchyard. The community would gather around for more Christmas hymns, a homily by the pastor, and then they would welcome in Christmas at midnight.

Katy patted Lucia's arm, then Glenn's shoulder, before leading Clover to his designated area where Joey would lead him to the church.

"May I lift you?" Miles nodded toward Glenn's back.

Lucia closed her eyes, tears threatening. Her heart hurt.

Before she could answer, a thudding of hooves had Glenn jerking against his reins and Miles pushing them both into the shelter of a building. Cows—ten, twenty of them—stampeded past. Shouts went up from the people gathered here at the center of town.

"What's happening?" Lucia gaped at the melee.

"That crazy Italian let them loose!" A young man ran after the cows, arms waving.

Miles and Lucia stared at one another. "Is Gio here?" she asked.

"He wouldn't cause this, but I aim to fix it. Stay here or he'll have my head."

It took all of a few minutes for the cows to thunder back the way they'd come, herded by a handful of farmers. Miles and Joey followed, the young man who'd accused Gio—or Lucia?—between them.

"Apologize." Joey shoved him toward Lucia.

The young man hung his head, long hair straggling over his face.

Miles cleared his throat. "Lucia, this is Alex Chiff. He wanted to break the truce and decided blaming it on the *foreigners* would be a smart idea. It wasn't."

"You're fortunate you didn't kill someone." Joey growled. "Now apologize before I kick your—before I take you to jail where the chief will make sure you have a pleasant Christmas."

"Fine," Alex mumbled. "I'm sorry."

"For?" Miles prompted.

"For blaming your kind."

"Of all the—" Joey yanked Alex around. "Maybe the ghosts of Christmas past, present, and future will all visit you tonight in your cell."

"You all right?" Miles squeezed Lucia's shoulder.

"I'm not sure I understand what happened."

"I'll have Lily tell you her story after Christmas brunch tomorrow. It'll fill in the details. Mrs. St. Thomas said we'll start as soon as you're ready, so ... ready to mount your stead?"

Lucia ran her hand over the donkey's nose again. "You ready to do this, Glenn?"

"*Scusa.* May I do the honor?"

Gio? She spun around.

He held his hat in his hands, hope and determination in his eyes.

"You're here." Not the most brilliant thing she'd ever said.

"Si, si. For you."

Miles clapped Gio on the shoulder and then disappeared into the night.

"I am sorry I left. I—"

The movement of the animals ahead of them warned them they needed to join the procession. Lucia allowed Gio to lift her to Glenn's back. As they progressed slowly down the street and all eyes turned toward them, Lucia's cheeks heated.

"I met Signora Gennaro." Gio spoke softly as he walked beside her. And then he told her of his meeting. Of how they came to an agreement to allow the women who wished to leave the madam's employ to go to the house of refuge Gio planned to build. The one he hoped Lucia would run.

"How did you get her to agree with you?" Lucia asked as he led her into the stable.

Gio tightened his grip on her hand. "*Amore ti fa' fare les cose piu' folle.*" Love makes you do the craziest things.

Love?

Unfortunately, the singing and service kept her from finding out what Gio meant by his statement. It was a strange sort of torture to pretend to be Gio's wife in front of an entire community while wondering if she really might be one day. It made her realize the answer to Katy's question, that she did want Gio. However, she also needed to know the future would not be a repeat of the past two weeks, of him pushing her away just when she felt closest to him.

The nearer to midnight they came, the harder it was to stay quiet. As the pastor led everyone in the singing of "Silent Night" to welcome in Christmas Day, Lucia couldn't wait any longer.

"What did you mean," she whispered, turning her head away from the people and then switching to Italian. "What did you mean when you said that about craziest things?"

"I thought escaping the tenements would bring freedom. I thought going to war would make me a hero. I thought doing good would make up for my mistakes. I thought keeping my heart hidden would save me from heartbreak. I thought wrong on all counts."

He clasped her mittened hand in his as the town's bell began to chime. Her heart pounded as loudly.

"Fear and peace, they are constantly at war, and I've decided to let peace win. God help me, I will from this day forward."

She stifled a sob as quiet tears slipped down her cheeks. She had her answer.

He tucked her into the crook of his arm as the twelfth bell signaled Christmas Day. The people around them shouted, "Merry Christmas!" At least, it sounded that way past the rushing in her ears as Gio bent his lips to hers. He pulled her closer, wrapping her in his arms as he kissed her soundly, breaking off too soon, to her mind. Except he trailed tiny kisses along her jaw until he whispered in her ear:

"*Ti amo*, Lucia Critelli." *I love you.*

Epilogue

Christmas Day

"So what are you going to do with the ring?" Lucia stood by Glenn's stall, feeding him a carrot.

Christmas morning had been spent with Lily's boisterous family and while Gio's own family gave *loud* its own definition, Lucia was sagging by the time the meal had ended. Now that they'd retreated to the quiet of Katy's barn for the afternoon, she seemed to be perking up. Gio studied her to be sure, contemplating an idea that screamed *too soon*, but in his heart, he had complete peace.

"Gio?" Lucia cocked her head and he realized he hadn't answered her question.

"I thought, it could buy the building, for the women's refuge."

Lucia rubbed the donkey's forelock. "I talked to Nonno. With his health declining, I'm not sure how many more years he'll be with us."

"Lucia." He squeezed her shoulder, hating to hear the grief lining her voice.

"He suggested we use our apartment. It's small, but it's in an immigrant neighborhood. It would feel like a home to them. Nonno could be the resident grandfather. You know how he took to Lily and Katy." Lucia finally raised her head, then looked away just as quickly. "I just don't know if it would work for ... well, never mind."

Maybe because God had just liberated him from his fears or maybe because of the memory of her kiss in that stable last night, or maybe because it was Christmas, Ugo's offer gave him a nudge toward his crazy idea.

"Do you think the women will be comfortable around you?" Lucia asked. "Most women are already, I suppose. Everyone loves you."

"And do you? Love me?" Gio ran a hand down her arm to capture her hand.

"I do, at that." A shy smile.

He tugged her to him. "And I love you."

A brighter smile.

Gio dropped to one knee and pulled the ring out of his pocket.

Lucia gave a tiny gasp.

"This ring, it is all I have—until we return to Chicago and I can give you Nonna's ring. It is a symbol of our future. Of working together. And opening the refuge for women. This ring will provide a place to welcome more women in need. That is mia bella, if you will make me *molto felice* and agree to be my wife. V*uoi sposarmi?*" *Will you marry me?*

Lucia's brown eyes lit up like starlight. "Si, si, Giouse. Yes to everything!"

Gio picked her up as he stood and went to spin her around only to have his ribs remind him that Ettore had broken a few of them. He hissed a breath and set her down.

"Are you all right?"

"Not romantic, these ribs." He gave a sheepish grin.

She rested her hand on his cheek. "They were broken for me."

He kissed her hand. "I would do it again."

She raised the ring to the sunlight. "What was intended as a gift, stolen for evil purposes, will now be used for good." She lifted her sparkling eyes to his. "I love you, Giosue Vella."

"What is keeping you two?" Miles poked his head inside the barn, bringing a cold breeze with him.

"If they're kissing, let's go." Joey's voice came from outside.

Gio grinned, slipped the ring on Lucia's finger, and waved her hand.

"Seriously?" Miles gaped, snowflakes resting on his wide shoulders. "I thought you planned to use your grandmother's—"

"The moment, I could not wait." Gio laughed. "Do you need advice on how to propose, mio amico?"

"You're planning to propose to my sister?" Joey followed Miles inside, shaking snow from his hat. "Staying on the force will mean I finally have enough to buy a ring for Katy."

"Aye, I have a ring." Miles grinned. "Perhaps a triple wedding?"

Joey glared at his likely future brother-in-law. "Not on your life, Wright. Lil and I share a birthday, no need to share a wedding."

Lucia buried her face in Gio's arm as her body shook with laughter.

Joy filled him. Here he was, surrounded by friends who sacrificed—and teased—like brothers and beside him was the most incredible woman, who agreed to spend the rest of her life with him. How could he not be happy the happiest man in America?

Gio hauled Lucia close, ignoring the protest in his ribs. "*Buon Natale!*"

Merry Christmas!

Author's Note

I'm so excited to write a story featuring two Italian-Americans! My paternal grandmother, the daughter of Italian immigrants, grew up in Chicago during the 1920s, and I grew up on her stories. While this tale has no parallel to her life, she fueled my love of this time in history.

What part of the story is based on true events? The opening prologue is based on an actual historical heist that ended with one of the robbers being gunned down in a Chicago alley from an apparent mob hit. You can read about the event on the North Carolina Department of Natural and Cultural Resources website: https://www.ncdcr.gov/blog/2014/11/15/charlotte-heist-foiled-1933. From there, my writer's imagination asked *why*, and the fictional diamond ring was born.

Al Capone, the notorious Chicago gangster, is also known for running soup kitchens during the Depression. You can read more on History.com: https://www.history.com/news/al-capone-great-depression-soup-kitchen. And, according to *Al Capone and the 1933 World's Fair: The End of the Gangster Era in Chicago* by William Elliott Hazelgrove (an informative book, though the language isn't PG), Al Capone did indeed fund church-hosted bread lines while in prison.

I love researching the history behind Christmas symbols, feasts, and festivals, so being able to include St. Nicholas Day and Santa

Lucia into this story was such fun. Both St. Nicholas and Saint Lucia were historical individuals, and the information I included in the story about their history is true. St. Nicholas is the figure from which Americans derived Santa Claus. Santa Lucia is commonly celebrated in Sweden, as her feast day coincides with what used to be the shortest and darkest day of the year. The celebration of light is still held today. However, in Italy, the feast day looks different, and in some cases, St. Lucia delivers gifts while riding a donkey. Lastly, according to the *Smithsonian* magazine, the first live nativity dates back to the thirteenth century.

Thank you for joining me for Gio and Lucia's story! If you enjoyed it, would you consider leaving an honest review on your preferred retail site to help other readers find *As Silent as the Night*? I'd also love to connect with you through my newsletter or social media. Please visit my website for all the applicable links at daniellegrandinetti.com.

My wish for you this Christmastime is that you will experience the peace that Gio discovers, the kind that casts out fear and replaces it with joy. This is the season we celebrate the hope that only Immanuel, God with Us, can give. And, as the angels said when Jesus was born: "Glory to God in the highest, and on earth peace, good will toward men." (Luke 2:14, KJV).

Merry Christmas!

Read the Whole Series

She came to America to escape a workhouse prison, but will the cost of freedom be too high a price to pay?

1933, Wisconsin--Large animal veterinarian Katy Wells takes her patients' welfare personally, so it's no surprise when she stands up to angry farmers planning a milk strike or takes in an injured draft horse to save its life. But after a visitor from the past discovers her location and reveals a threat, she must choose between her work and her freedom, and whether to trust a man to keep her safe.

For details, please visit
daniellegrandinetti.com/to-stand-in-the-breach

She's fiercely independent. He's determined to protect her.

Wisconsin, 1933—When a routine mission becomes an ambush that kills his team, Craft Agency sniper Miles Wright determines to find the persons responsible and protect the woman he rescued. But the fierce independence that led Lily Moore to leave her family's dairy business for the solitary life of a dog trainer and the isolation of her farm don't make that easy. Neither does his unwanted attraction to her. Meanwhile, escalating incidents confirm that she's far from safe.

Lily fears letting the surprisingly gentle retired marine into her life almost as much as she fears whoever is threatening her. As Wisconsin farmers edge toward another milk strike, one that will surely turn violent, it becomes clear that the plot against Lily may be part of a much larger conspiracy. When the search for her abductor leads close to home, she must decide whether to trust her family or the man who saved her life.

For details, please visit
daniellegrandinetti.com/a-strike-to-the-heart

Coming March 2023

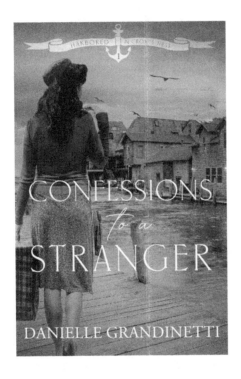

**She's lost her future. He's sacrificed his. Now they have a chance
to reclaim it—together.**

Wisconsin, 1930—While fleeing for her life, Adaleigh Sirland's rescue
of a child introduces her to a family who provides her safe harbor.
When her identity comes under threat of exposure, she must choose

between running once more or helping the man who teaches her to hope again.

First mate David Martins is intrigued by the mysterious woman taken in by his grandmother, but she wrestles with a troubled past. When his estranged father is arrested for murder, can David put aside his own struggles in time to discern which secret threatens Adaleigh before it kills them both?

Welcome to Crow's Nest,
where danger and romance meet at the water's edge.

For more information about *Confessions to a Stranger*,
including purchase links, please visit
daniellegrandinetti.com/confessions-to-a-stranger

About the Author

Danielle Grandinetti is a historical romantic suspense author and a book blogger at *DaniellesWritingSpot.com*. Her books include *To Stand in the Breach* and *A Strike to the Heart*, her short stories have appeared in several publications, and her writing has won the University of Northwestern Distinguished Faith in Writing Award. Originally from the Chicagoland area, she now lives along Lake Michigan's Wisconsin shoreline with her husband and their two young sons. Danielle especially loves quiet mornings served with the perfect cup of tea.

Made in the USA
Monee, IL
18 September 2022